S0-BFF-605

She risked nudging the door open and looked in.

Justin lay in a shaft of moonlight. Nervous, yet unable to stop herself, Sarah slipped in and knelt beside him, her face only a few inches from his. She was free now to look with longing.

She felt like a thief, stealing her joy from a defenseless man, but she couldn't help it. After the long, lonely months, nothing could have stopped her from taking this moment. Perhaps it was all she would ever have.

"I love you," she whispered. "I never stopped loving you. I never will."

Justin stirred, and she rose quickly and fled. In her room, her son Nicky had just awakened. Sarah scooped him up and held him tightly to her.

"He's come back to us, my darling," she whispered. "Do you hear that? He's come back to us."

Dear Reader,

As the long summer stretches before us, July sizzles with an enticing Special Edition lineup!

We begin with this month's THAT SPECIAL WOMAN! title brought to you by the wonderful Jennifer Greene. She concludes her STANFORD SISTERS series with *The 200% Wife*—an engaging story about one woman's quest to be the very best at everything, most especially love.

If you delight in marriage-of-convenience stories that evolve into unexpected love, be sure to check out *Mail-Order Matty* by Emilie Richards, book one in our FROM BUD TO BLOSSOM theme series. Written by four popular authors, this brand-new series contains magical love stories that bring change to the characters' lives when they least expect it.

Pull out your handkerchiefs, because we have a three-hankie Special Edition novel that will touch you unlike any of the stories you've experienced before. *Nothing Short of a Miracle* by Patricia Thayer is a poignant story about a resilient woman, a devoted father and a cherished son who yearn for a miracle—and learn to trust in the wondrous power of love.

If absorbing amnesia stories are your forte, be sure to check out *Forgotten Fiancée* by Lucy Gordon. Or perhaps you can't pass up an engrossing family drama with a seductive twist. Then don't miss out on *The Ready-Made Family* by Laurie Paige. Finally, we wrap up a month of irresistible romance when one love-smitten heroine impulsively poses as her twin sister and marries the man of her dreams in *Substitute Bride* by Trisha Alexander.

An entire summer of romance is just beginning to unfold at Special Edition! I hope you enjoy each and every story to come!

Sincerely,

Tara Gavin,
Senior Editor

Please address questions and book requests to:
Silhouette Reader Service
U.S.: 3010 Walden Ave., P.O. Box 1325, Buffalo, NY 14269
Canadian: P.O. Box 609, Fort Erie, Ont. L2A 5X3

LUCY GORDON

FORGOTTEN FIANCÉE

Silhouette®

SPECIAL ✦ EDITION®

Published by Silhouette Books

America's Publisher of Contemporary Romance

If you purchased this book without a cover you should be aware that this book is stolen property. It was reported as "unsold and destroyed" to the publisher, and neither the author nor the publisher has received any payment for this "stripped book."

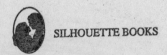

SILHOUETTE BOOKS

ISBN 0-373-24112-7

FORGOTTEN FIANCÉE

Copyright © 1997 by Lucy Gordon

All rights reserved. Except for use in any review, the reproduction or utilization of this work in whole or in part in any form by any electronic, mechanical or other means, now known or hereafter invented, including xerography, photocopying and recording, or in any information storage or retrieval system, is forbidden without the written permission of the editorial office, Silhouette Books, 300 East 42nd Street, New York, NY 10017 U.S.A.

All characters in this book have no existence outside the imagination of the author and have no relation whatsoever to anyone bearing the same name or names. They are not even distantly inspired by any individual known or unknown to the author, and all incidents are pure invention.

This edition published by arrangement with Harlequin Books S.A.

® and TM are trademarks of Harlequin Books S.A., used under license. Trademarks indicated with ® are registered in the United States Patent and Trademark Office, the Canadian Trade Marks Office and in other countries.

Printed in U.S.A.

LUCY GORDON

met her husband-to-be in Venice, fell in love the first evening
and got engaged two days later. They're still happily married
and now live in England with their three dogs. For twelve
years Lucy was a writer for an English women's magazine.
She interviewed many of the world's most interesting men,
including Warren Beatty, Richard Chamberlain, Sir Roger
Moore, Sir Alec Guinness and Sir John Gielgud.

In 1985 she won the *Romantic Times* Reviewers' Choice
Award for Outstanding Series Romance Author. She has also
won a Golden Leaf Award from the New Jersey Chapter of
RWA, was a finalist in the RWA Golden Medallion contest in
1988 and won the 1990 RITA Award in the Best Traditional
Romance category for *Song of the Lorelei*.

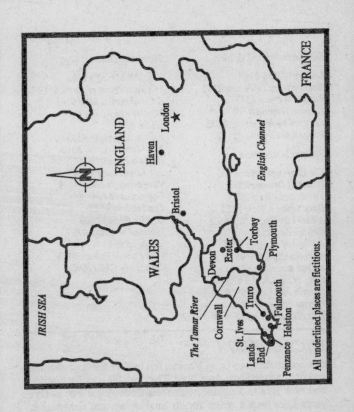

IRISH SEA

WALES

ENGLAND

Bristol •

Haven •

London ★

N

Devon

Exeter •

Torbay

Plymouth

The Tamar River

Cornwall

Truro

Falmouth

St. Ives

Lands End

Penzance Helston

English Channel

FRANCE

All underlined places are fictitious.

Prologue

It had been a long, troubled night, but in the morning her son lay in her arms, and pain was forgotten. Like any new baby he had features that were smudged and uncertain, but even now Sarah could see in them the face of the man she loved and would never see again.

"He's a fine little fellow." Uncle Nick leaned over, and Sarah turned so that he could get his first view of his new relative. "He's got the Mottson nose," he declared with satisfaction.

"Uncle Nick," she protested with a faint laugh. "He's three hours old."

"That's the thing about the Mottson nose. You can see it right from the start."

She smiled and let it go. The old man, who was actually her great-uncle, had taken her in when she had nowhere else to turn. He'd allowed his life to be disrupted without complaint, and she would let him see whatever he liked in his great-great-nephew.

"Thought of a name yet?" Nick asked.

"Justin Nicholas," Sarah whispered. "And we'll call him Nicky."

Uncle Nick beamed at the compliment. "That's— that's just—well, I don't know."

"You've earned it," she said. "I don't know what I'd have done without you."

"Now, don't talk foolishness. Who else would you have come to but your old uncle?" His face became grave suddenly. "Is—is there anyone you'd like me to get in touch with?"

"No one," Sarah said without hesitation. "No one at all."

"Darling, I've never bothered you about the man before—not when I saw you didn't want to talk about him. But whoever he is, he's just become a father, and he has a right to know."

Sarah shook her head stubbornly.

"Is he married?" Nick asked gently.

"No."

"He's not dead, is he?"

"No, he's not dead."

"Then he ought to know that he's got a son."

"You don't understand," she cried. "He doesn't *want* to know." She kissed her baby in a passion of tenderness while tears poured down her cheeks onto the child. "He doesn't want us," she sobbed. *"He doesn't want us."*

Chapter One

"I'm afraid Mr. Hallwood is rather busy—"

"He won't be too busy for me. I'll show myself in."

Justin grinned at the sound of Marguerite's confident voice. Normally he disliked being disturbed at work, but today was her birthday, and he was feeling indulgent. He was pleased by her flaunted beauty and pleased with himself for choosing her as his prospective wife. She was the best, and he always bought the best.

"Darling, when are you going to tell that dragon to stop trying to keep me out?" she said, almost purring, gliding across the floor to envelop him in a perfumed embrace. She wore a mink coat, for it was March and still chilly.

"Perhaps she thinks I have important work to do?" he suggested.

"More important than me?"

"Nothing's more important than you," he said automatically, and was rewarded with a kiss.

"I hope I'm going to get my present now?" she asked.

"Not until later." She made a little moue of disappointment. "All right, you can have one of them." He gave her a small black box. "I saw it in Cartier's, and it made me think of you."

The box contained a very large diamond brooch. Marguerite's smile wavered for a fraction of a second before she voiced her delight. "Darling, it's beautiful—"

"It's not your main present. You'll get that this evening at the party."

"I can't wait for you to see my dress. I had it specially made, and it cost a fortune."

"So I should hope. I want you to do me proud."

"Have I ever disappointed you?"

For some reason the right words wouldn't come. "You're always—exactly what I expect," was the best he could manage.

She laughed, evidently seeing nothing amiss in this lukewarm tribute. "It's nice to know I give satisfaction," she said with a trill. "Now I must fly. Don't be late for the party."

When she'd gone Justin sat for a moment, wondering why he'd bought a brooch instead of the engagement ring she so plainly expected. He planned to marry her. He should have proposed by now, but something he didn't understand always held him back. He would ask her tonight—or perhaps tomorrow.

But he'd been saying that to himself for two weeks, he realized. It wasn't like him to be indecisive.

He rubbed his eyes, trying to shift the metal band that seemed to have tightened around his head. It wasn't exactly a headache, more a general feeling of stifling imprisonment. It had troubled him a lot recently, and he didn't know why.

If ever a man had a rich, satisfying life, that man was Justin Hallwood. At thirty-seven he was in his prime, heading a firm that was doing spectacularly well. The clothes he wore, the food he ate, the car he drove were the best, the most costly. The same was true of Marguerite. When he walked into a fashionable restaurant with her on his arm he knew that heads turned and murmurs of envy pursued them. He was a man beloved of the gods.

Why then this persistent feeling of malaise, of discontent that sometimes verged on actual despair? No! He cut off the thought. That was a fanciful way of thinking, and he had no time for what was fanciful. It was stern realism and long hours of hard work that had enabled him to build up Hallwood Construction and Engineering until it was one of the largest firms of its kind in the country. He only wished his younger brother, Greg, would understand that, and take a more serious interest in business.

Greg himself chanced to look in at that moment with some papers. He was a good-looking, lively young man. "I've had Foster's on the phone," he said, a tad too casually.

"I don't want to hear it."

"Hell, Justin! What would be so terrible about giving them another couple of months to pay?"

"You said that last time, and the time before. I listened to you and what happened? When payment day arrived there were more excuses."

"Well, how do you expect them to raise the money when we've stolen most of their business?"

Justin's sharp blue eyes gained a frosty look that his brother knew and dreaded. "We stole nothing," he snapped. "Their customers chose us because of our greater efficiency and competitive prices."

"Meaning that we used our size and strength to undercut them, knowing that they couldn't fight back?"

"Business is business! It's a hard world."

"I'll bet our prices shoot up again once we've closed Foster's."

"They've had all the time I'm prepared to give them."

"I just can't tell old man Foster that."

"All right, I'll talk to him myself. Though how you're going to survive in this world if you can't steel yourself for unpleasant jobs I can't imagine."

"Justin, please—"

"Is there anything more for me to sign? No? Good. Don't forget we have a meeting with the auditors at five this afternoon. Come fully prepared."

"What about Marguerite's party?"

"It doesn't start until eight. Forget the party until you've done some more work."

"Wait until you see my date. She's a real eye-catcher."

"I'm sure she was chosen for looks, like all your lady friends," Justin said dryly.

"Coming from the man who walked off with the gorgeous Marguerite, that's a bit rich," Greg complained. "Are you going to announce the wedding tonight, by the way?"

"That's none of your concern," Justin said with a sudden sharpness.

"Everyone thinks it's going to happen and that's why you're holding the party at Jaquino's."

"Marguerite chose Jaquino's, not me."

"That's not how she tells it. According to her it's something sentimental about your first meeting. Didn't you meet her the night of the Carter Vernon reception?"

"No, three weeks earlier. She was dating Vernon, and I met him with her a couple of times."

"But he brought her to that reception, didn't he? And you and she looked at each other across a crowded room—"

"Have you been drinking?" Justin asked coldly.

"All right, only a joke. Anyway, Marguerite has happy memories of Jaquino's. Did you and she finish that evening together? I remember hearing someone say you'd driven off with a woman—"

"I'm sure you have work to do," Justin interrupted him. "Next time you want to indulge your frivolous ramblings, please do it somewhere else."

Greg knew that chilly tone. He took the signed papers and left quietly. In the anteroom he raised his eyes to heaven for the benefit of Justin's secretary.

Justin called her on the intercom a moment later. "Hold my calls," he said curtly.

He couldn't explain his sudden need to be alone. It would have been a weakness to admit that he was unsettled by Greg's words. That night at Jaquino's had been two years ago. It was over, done with.

No, not done with. It would never be done with until he knew what had become of Sarah Conroy and the child she'd carried. *His* child.

He'd met her at the reception to celebrate his taking over Carter Vernon. Officially the two firms had merged, but everyone had known that the Hallwood power had overcome the smaller business. Edward Carter had looked sad at the end of his life's work, and Justin had felt impatient. The man had just made a handsome profit.

Jack Vernon had turned up with his fiancée, as he insisted on calling Marguerite, with more optimism than confidence. Since the takeover he was a loser, and Marguerite's eyes were straying toward Justin. He'd danced with her a couple of times that night but ignored her hints that they leave together.

He could still remember his first sight of the young woman standing alone by the wall. She stood out with her face that wore only a touch of makeup and her glossy dark brown hair that looked as if she'd just run a comb through it. Her dress was simple, not couture simple but the plain garment of someone who could afford no better. She looked fresh and natural, and suddenly Justin found the noise and the smoke irksome. He made his way across to her and shouted over the din, "You don't look as if you're enjoying it much."

"Oh, yes—yes, I am," she began valiantly, but the pretense soon collapsed. "This isn't really my sort of scene."

"Nor mine," he said wryly. "How did you get roped in?"

She was with her boyfriend, who worked for Hallwood. There was no sign of the boyfriend until Justin spotted him dancing smoothly with someone else. The young woman smiled and insisted that she was fine—just fine, honestly. Justin turned to speak to someone who was trying to claim his attention, and when he looked around she was gone.

He saw her again at the end of the evening, standing outside looking as though her hopes were fast fading. "He's gone," Justin told her. "He went off with that painted piece he was dancing with. You're better off without him."

"I did warn him that I'd be out of place. He must have realized I was right." She spoke without self-pity, and Justin regarded her with interest.

"Where do you live?" When she told him he whistled. "You won't get back there without help. I'll drive you."

"I can get a bus—"

"I'll drive you," he said firmly.

He could sense her unease at being in his luxurious car. Her tiny apartment was at the end of a long, bleak road, the kind he'd lived in as a boy and fought to escape. At the door she began to thank him, but he invited himself in. He was curious to see how she lived.

Her two little rooms surprised him. Despite the dreariness of her surroundings they were bright and cheerful. There were flowers everywhere, some real, some photographs on the wall, some her own drawings. She made him coffee, and as they drank they exchanged names. Hers was Sarah Conroy, and it struck him as like herself, down-to-earth, good and honest. She was in her mid-twenties, but she had a shyness and lack of sophistication that was a novelty to him and that made her seem younger.

"By the way, I'm Justin Hallwood," he said.

"Yes, I know. I saw you when they made the speeches. I'm sorry if I said anything I shouldn't have before. I didn't realize you were Philip's boss!"

"Philip, I take it, is your ex-boyfriend."

"My *ex*-boyfriend?"

"Of course he is, after the way he abandoned you tonight. You can't go on seeing him."

He spoke peremptorily and was rather annoyed when she laughed. But after a moment he laughed, too.

She made sandwiches, and later he decided it had been guilt that made him invite her to dinner. She was so poor and feeding him must have depleted her food stock. But the truth was that he wanted to see her again. She was fresh and original, and she could make him laugh, especially when she was innocently tactless, which was often.

"Oh, heavens, there's another of my clangers," she would say, covering her mouth and looking like a guilty schoolgirl.

He would grin and swear that he enjoyed her clangers. It was true enough, but the thought flashed through his mind that it was lucky they were alone. It wouldn't do to have her dropping bricks over the feet of his clients.

He began calling her, taking her out, and at last they became lovers.

Strange that he should use the word *lovers* when he never used it of himself and the woman he now planned to marry. He was welcome in Marguerite's bed whenever he wanted. His expensive gifts had ensured that. She was a good sexual partner who knew how to excite a man. Yet he'd never thought of her as a lover.

Sarah Conroy had been his lover because she loved him. He knew it from the warmth and generosity of her passion. He'd never said he loved her, either to himself or to her. But she charmed him, and he could talk to her. Perhaps it didn't suit him to look more closely at his own feelings.

Mostly their nights were spent at his apartment, but one evening she cried off their date, pleading a heavy cold.

"I'll come and see you," he said at once.

"No, no, you mustn't. Remember how easily you catch cold."

"How did you know that?" he demanded, displeased.

"You told me the first evening. You said you were always the first to catch any cold that was going around."

He wondered what had possessed him to reveal his

one weakness. He'd always kept it a closely guarded secret, because in the jungle you didn't dare reveal the slightest chink in your defenses. But there was a warmth and sympathy about her that lured a man to talk.

He visited her that night, and she greeted him from behind a large handkerchief. "Go away, I'm full of germs," she protested in a muffled voice.

He settled her on the sofa and made her a supper of tea and poached eggs. Then he tidied up with a deftness that surprised her.

"My mother was a tidy woman, and she had a heavy hand," he explained. "I soon learned to do as I was told."

She laughed and had a coughing fit.

"Come out from behind that hanky," he said.

"I've got a red nose," she wailed.

"Let me see."

"No, I look awful."

He'd prevailed at last. Her nose was very red, and her eyes looked heavy. But it didn't cross his mind that she was unattractive. She was his delightful Sarah, especially when, a moment later, she dropped one of her clangers.

"I can't imagine you with a mother," she said serenely, then clapped her hand to her mouth. "Oh, no, I didn't mean that exactly—"

"Yes, you did." He grinned. "An ogre, generated from inside a machine. Is that me?"

"Oh, you know what I mean."

He'd told her about his boyhood with the feckless

father who was always on the verge of making his
fortune, although seldom in work.

''I grew sick of listening to his endless daydreaming
while my mother scrimped and saved because he'd
spent what little money we had on one mad scheme
after another. I was determined to get out and take
Greg with me. I'm only sorry my mother didn't live
long enough for me to give her some comfort.''

Her own childhood had been happier. She'd grown
up in a small country village with her mother and her
great-uncle.

''Mom died four years ago. Haven is such a sleepy
little place. I wanted to find out if the city streets really
were paved with gold.''

He hardly heard her words. He was watching her,
enjoying the comfortable glow that was pervading
him. He hadn't felt like this since he was a boy, sitting
at the kitchen table doing his homework, hearing his
mother's movements in the background, knowing that
the world was a good place because she was there.

He hadn't stayed long. He'd seen her safely to bed
and departed, smiling. He'd paid for that visit with one
of the worst colds he'd ever had, and yet the evening
stood out in his mind as an oasis of warmth and contentment.

When had he first sensed something wrong? Perhaps it was when she refused to accept the fur stole
he'd bought her. She hated the whole idea of fur, and
she wouldn't budge. Until then he'd known only her
gentle side, but she had displayed a stubbornness that
surprised and displeased him.

But the real trouble had started the night he'd told

her about the little company he'd managed to close down by getting control of its debts. The owner had fought to the last ditch but had finally admitted defeat. It was another victory for Justin Hallwood, but Sarah had only said, "It must be dreadful to lose everything like that!"

Her words had jarred him. This wasn't how she was supposed to respond to the tale of his triumph. "The place was a millstone around the man's neck," he said impatiently. "He ought to be glad to be rid of it. I've made him a generous offer."

"An offer he couldn't refuse," she replied wryly.

His face tightened. "That was quite unnecessary."

"It was only a little joke, Justin."

"In very poor taste."

"You're right. It isn't funny, at all. It's terribly sad for that poor man, after he'd worked all those years—"

"Sarah, you're looking at this the wrong way. In business you need a grand vision, or you'll always be stumbling around over minor details."

"And that's all the little people are?" she asked, looking at him strangely. "Minor details that don't matter?"

"Of course they matter," he said impatiently. "I'm not a monster. I don't throw them out to starve. I told you I made a generous offer."

"But you took away that man's pride and joy. Maybe you starved his heart."

He found this remark so fantastic that he could only stare. But after a moment's intense annoyance he forgave her. After all, what could she know?

"The point is," he said, "that I have a vision for my firm. I started it from nothing. There were plenty of people who tried to put me out of business with some very dirty tricks. I didn't complain. I just fought back. Now it's on course to dominate the market in this country, and I won't stop until it dominates the world market."

"Dominates the world," she mused thoughtfully. "Justin, how many small people will you have to crush to achieve that?"

He sighed and gave up trying to explain what she couldn't understand. "In the end, the world boils down to the small people and the big people," he declared bluntly. "I've tried being both, and I know which kind I want to be."

"But—"

"Another coffee?" he asked smoothly, bored with this kind of talk. He didn't take her out so she could criticise him.

Later that night he'd made love to her skillfully, caressing her in the ways he knew she loved and reveling in the passionate response of her eager body. But again he felt something wrong, and at last he realized that her eyes were closed. Usually she made love looking at him, but now she was shutting him out.

They'd stayed together for a little longer, trying to pretend that all was well. But he never again spoke to her of his work, and it irked him to recognize that he flinched before her judgment. He began to be angry with her.

There was no quarrel, but one night he dropped her

at her door and said, "I'll be busy for a while. I'll call you in a week or so."

"All right," she said softly. "Goodbye, Justin."

She smiled at him, and it was the gallant smile he'd seen the first night. She knew she was being brushed off. Perhaps she even knew it was because her honesty unnerved him. But she was without self-pity, accepting her happiness as a gift and refusing to complain when it was over. There was a pain in the area of his heart, but he ignored it.

Several times over the next three weeks he'd almost called her, but what would have been the point? They wouldn't have suited each other long-term. He needed a wife who would be a part of his professional world, as Sarah never could. It was better this way.

But then she'd turned up at his apartment one evening and told him she was expecting a child. And he'd said the first thing that came into his head. "Don't worry. I'll take care of you."

When he saw her radiant smile he realized that she'd misunderstood. "I mean I'll find you the best clinic there is. It's a simple operation these days, and of course I'll pay for everything..." As her smile died he found he couldn't go on. A moment before she'd been glorified, treasuring the most wonderful gift in the world. Now her face showed only disbelieving horror.

"Kill our baby," she whispered. "That's what you mean, don't you?"

Dismay had made him speak roughly. "It's not exactly a baby yet—"

"It is to me," she burst out fiercely. "It's a living

child, *my* child! Yours, too, if you'd wanted it. But it's nothing to you, is it? Just an inconvenience to be disposed of.''

He turned away from the accusation in her eyes, but she came after him. ''Justin, I didn't come here to trap you. I came because you had the right to know you're going to be a father. I'm not asking you to marry me. I don't even *want* to marry you if you don't love me. But don't ask me to kill your child.''

She'd made it easy for him. He could have squared his conscience with a financial settlement. But the devil seemed to have gotten into him, and it maddened him that she wouldn't see things his way.

''For heaven's sake!'' he shouted. ''Stop using emotive words. It's not a child or a baby. Just a fetus. It's about the size of a pinhead, and easy to get rid of.''

''I'm not going to get rid of my baby,'' she said. ''I've done what I had to do in coming here, but it's over. You needn't think about us anymore.''

''Do be sensible,'' he begged irritably. ''I told you I'd take care of everything, and I will. I don't shirk my responsibilities.''

''Oh, but you do, Justin. That's exactly what you're doing. You've created life, but you don't want to be responsible for it. And I think maybe I'm glad. Because now I'm finished with you. I loved you. I know you can be hard and unkind, but I thought there was a good man underneath. But I was wrong. I don't want you for the father of my child. You aren't fit to be a father.''

''That's enough!'' he roared, turning away from her

and slamming his hand down on a table. He stayed like that for a full minute, calming himself, hoping she wouldn't goad him further. He glanced up and saw her face reflected in the mirror. She was distraught, tears pouring down her cheeks. He closed his eyes against the sight. He didn't know what had happened to him. He hated himself but couldn't stop. When he felt he was in control again he turned with kinder words on his lips.

She was gone.

Justin rushed to the door and looked into the corridor. It was empty. There was no sign of her. He leaped into an elevator, cursing with impatience as it descended to the first floor. Someone told him that a young woman had left a moment ago and vanished into the crowd.

He tried to contact her at her little flat, at her place of work, but she'd left them both that same day. He wrote to her, hoping she'd arranged for her mail to be redirected, but his letters came back. He hired a firm of private investigators, but they failed, partly because Justin could give them nothing to go on. He thought Sarah had mentioned a place she'd once lived, but the name had gone out of his head.

In desperation he consulted Philip, but Philip, knowing only that his ex had taken up with the boss, decided that safety lay in ignorance. "I didn't really know her all that well," he insisted.

"Didn't she ever tell you where she lived before she came to London?" Justin demanded.

"Somewhere in the country?" Philip hazarded.

"Look, I hardly knew her." He wouldn't budge from this.

Sarah had vanished into thin air, leaving behind only her last terrible words. "I don't want you for the father of my child. You aren't fit to be a father."

"We'll have to come out here for a while," Sarah said to her son, smiling into his big round eyes. "Uncle Nick wants to finish the icing on your cake. This is a big day for you, your very first birthday. How about that?"

The baby chuckled, not because he understood but because he chuckled at everything. Life was a constant delight to him. His mother hugged him against her, overwhelmed with love for this merry scrap who felt so warm and sweet in her arms.

"We're going to have a party," she went on, "with presents and balloons, and all your friends. Why don't we see if we can find some wildflowers to put around the house?"

She climbed the gentle hill that rose behind the village of Haven. The first signs of spring were just appearing. Buds adorned the trees, and the landscape was yellow with daffodils.

Sarah sat on the ground with Nicky between her knees and drank in the beauty. It had been a hard winter, and the March winds still blew, but the sun was out. Down below she could see the houses, and there was the main street along which she'd hurried on that desperate night, not knowing if Uncle Nick would take her in. He belonged to the old school, which made harsh judgments of unmarried mothers.

There was Mottson's General Store, the little shop that had been his life for forty years. She could just make out the side door where she'd knocked. He'd opened it at once, drawing her in out of the rain and hugging her.

The old man had been sad about her pregnancy but not censorious. He'd asked about the father but respected her refusal to speak of him. And he'd made it clear that this was her home. The most critical thing he'd said was, "You should never have left the country. You don't belong in the city any more than I do. Bad things happen there."

She'd nodded, but in her heart she knew she could never regret those few blazing weeks of joy. She'd loved Justin. He hadn't loved her, and in the end he'd broken her heart. But the beauty had been fierce and wonderful while it lasted, and it had left her with a miracle.

At first glance Nicky didn't look like his father. But his eyes were the same startling blue, and his pudgy, infant hands already showed signs of the long fingers he'd inherited from Justin. Sarah splayed one of the little hands lovingly in hers. She'd thought she could never be happy again, but at this moment, sitting on the quiet hillside, listening to the birdsong, she knew that she was blessed. It was he who'd lost everything.

She and Nicky returned home, their hands filled with violets and buttercups. Uncle Nick had finished the icing on the cake, and even if it was a little wonky, it was still a masterpiece. In the center stood one large candle.

There were eight guests, aged from one to three,

accompanied by mothers, aunts or grandparents. There were balloons and paper hats, and a box of crackers Uncle Nick had kept from Christmas. Somebody's grandfather did conjuring tricks and got them all wrong, but nobody minded. Sarah opened presents and showed them to her little son, who gave his fat chuckle to every one and happily tore up the wrapping paper.

There were jellies and ice creams for tea. Then Sarah lit the candle and showed Nicky how to blow. He puffed up his cheeks, but the flame only wavered. It took a huge gust from everyone to put it out, while Nicky waved his arms and crowed approval. A final rendering of "Happy Birthday" and the party was over.

Just before she put Nicky to bed Sarah held him up to the window. "Look," she said eagerly, "there's a shooting star. Let's each make a wish. Anything you like." Nicky gurgled gleefully and reached out his hands. "I know," she said tenderly. "You want the whole of life, and you'll have everything I can give you, my darling—except one thing."

Now she knew what her own wish would be. It wasn't for Nicky, who already had so much. It was for the man who had nothing in the midst of riches.

"I want a miracle," she whispered, "so that he can understand, before it's too late for him."

As always, Marguerite did Justin credit. The black, glittering dress clung to her voluptuous figure. The neck was so low as to be barely decent, showing off the pearly whiteness of her shoulders and bosom. With her golden hair piled on her head she looked what she was, a hard, glossy woman who'd groomed herself to be the wife of a rich man. There was applause as she walked in on his arm.

The guests were arranged around small tables, with a long table at one end, where Justin and Marguerite would sit with the more notable guests. He led her to the spot, while the band played and everyone sang "Happy Birthday" and she blew kisses. An onlooker might have thought her overcome with surprise, although she'd overseen the arrangements herself, with a steely eye for detail. Justin had attended dinner parties in her home and knew that she was a superb hostess, skilled in *cordon bleu* cookery and abreast of the latest topics of conversation. She would be an excellent wife for a man like him.

"Darling," Marguerite cooed, "you shouldn't have done all this for me."

"You deserve only the best," he said gallantly.

As ill luck would have it, they were placed near the spot he'd seen Sarah standing two years ago. Justin cursed Greg and his unruly tongue. The last person he wanted to think of tonight was Sarah, with all the associations of failure and guilt she brought with her.

He'd worked hard at banishing those thoughts. He'd told himself how unreasonable she was to have vanished without giving him a chance to explain. But there was a shadow on his heart that wouldn't go away. She'd been worth ten of the glamorous dolls he normally escorted. He knew that. He'd known it on the day he defiantly decided to marry a woman who was the very opposite of Sarah.

He turned to that woman now, seeking reassurance

in her showy beauty, her perfect grooming, her *suitability*. She smiled at him, but her smile was all wrong. It glittered with triumph. A woman's smile should be gentle and glowing, full of love, making a man feel like a king.

"Are we ready to start?" he asked harshly. He was afraid his unease might show, but he needn't have worried. Marguerite noticed nothing beyond her own immediate concerns.

Course by course, the perfect meal was served. Justin drank wine, cracked jokes, flirted with Marguerite and longed for the evening to end.

When they reached the coffee and liqueur stage the waiters carried in a huge cake, lavishly decorated in white sugar and adorned with a tactful twenty candles. Justin rose and made an elegant speech. Marguerite listened to him with an air of expectancy.

"I couldn't bring your birthday gift in here because it's too large," he said. "And so—" At his signal the dark blue curtains behind him parted, revealing a screen. A video was running, showing a sleek, glossy sports car. The guests oohed and aahed with admiration. Justin presented Marguerite with the keys, and she threw her arms around his neck, apparently overcome with joy. But at the last second he saw her eyes, filled with cold fury at receiving a car and not the engagement ring she'd wanted.

As the party broke up Greg murmured to his brother, "You were expected to propose, you know. She's mad as fire that you didn't."

"I'll propose in my own good time," Justin snapped, "and not in front of a crowd."

"Ah, so it's shyness that held you back," Greg said, grinning wickedly. "I wondered what it was."

"Mind your own damned business!"

Marguerite made a splendid show of delight, insisting on going outside to see "my darling present from my darling man." She exclaimed over the beautiful vehicle with little screams of ecstasy, then slid into the driving seat and started the engine, which purred as softly as a kitten. "It's the most gorgeous car," she said. "Thank you, *dearest* Justin."

"It'll be delivered to your home tomorrow," he said.

"But I must just drive it for a few minutes now."

"Better wait. It's very late and—"

"But I *want* to drive it. Don't spoil my birthday, darling."

She began to ease the car onto the road. With an oath Justin vaulted into the passenger seat. "Just a few minutes, then," he said. "Luckily the road's empty— hey! What are you doing?"

"Putting her through her paces."

"For God's sake, Marguerite! You can't do this speed in a built-up area. Slow down. Let me take the wheel."

Her answer was to slam her foot down, venting her temper on the accelerator. Justin held his breath, praying that nothing would appear in their path. He knew better than to try to snatch the wheel, but he shouted at her to slow down.

"Don't be a spoilsport," she cried. "I'm enjoying your lovely gift. Don't you want me to have fun?"

"Not by getting us both killed," he said grimly. "Look out!"

A car had appeared from a side street. Marguerite had had just enough champagne to slow her reactions. She swore and wrenched at the wheel, turning the car sideways with a violence that threw it into a skid. Justin's last view was of the street whirling around him before a lamppost appeared by his window, and the side of the car slammed into it.

His head ached, and the light hurt his eyes. The nurse by his bed vanished as soon as he awoke, returning with a doctor, who said, "That's right. I knew you'd come back soon. It's about time."

"I feel awful," Justin said thickly.

"You will for a while. You've been out for three days."

"What happened?"

"You were in a car crash. You came off badly because the car hit the lamppost on your side. Luckily the lady got thrown clear, and she has only minor cuts and bruises."

Justin fought to clear his head. "I need to see my brother."

"He's just outside. I'll get him."

Greg's face was tense with strain. "You gave us a fright."

Justin managed a grin. "Never fear," he said huskily. "I'll be around to hassle you for a long time yet. Look, the doctor says I've been out for three days. I'm still a bit groggy, so fill me in. He said there was a woman in the car with me—"

"Marguerite."

"What was I doing with her?"

"She wanted to drive her new car. Don't you remember?"

"No, my mind's a blank just before the accident."

"Well, the whole thing was her fault, and I told her so."

"You shouldn't have done that, not until the reception's over, anyway. Obviously I'm not going to be there, so you'll have to—"

"Wait a minute!" Greg leaned over him, frowning with concern. "What reception?"

"The Carter Vernon reception, of course, to mark the takeover."

"But—that was two years ago."

Justin stared at him. "Two years ago? What the devil are you talking about? It's tomorrow."

Chapter Two

"Sure you'll be all right while I'm gone?"

"Uncle Nick," Sarah protested, laughing. "We'll be fine. Anyone would think we'd never looked after the shop before."

"It's not the shop I worry about. It's you two, all on your own tonight. Burglars and all."

"Haven's had one burglary in the last two years. And that was only Joker breaking into the newsagent because one of his school friends dared him."

"Just the same, be sure you lock up properly. Perhaps I shouldn't go away—"

"We'll manage for one night," she assured him.

"Give Nicky that little rubber duck at bath time. He likes to splash about."

"You'll be telling me how to change his diapers next. Will you stop fretting?"

"Okay, okay, I'm an old fusspot. I know it without anyone telling me."

"Go on and have fun," she commanded him. "And bring back something beautiful."

"I will. I'm going to hit the jackpot this time, you'll see."

He departed at last. Sarah stood in the doorway with her little son in her arms, and together they waved as the old man got into the ancient car and drove away.

"He thinks we can't manage without him," she said, kissing Nicky. "But we can look after each other, can't we? Mmm, you smell gorgeous."

She settled him down into the playpen that took up a corner of the little shop, making it even more crowded than usual. Mottson's General Store served Haven with groceries, hardware and anything else that other shops didn't bother to stock, and it was a tight squeeze.

The village was bathed in the warmth of early summer, and Sarah pulled the door wide open. Nicky was earnestly placing building blocks one on top of another. Now and then the pile would topple over, but he was never fazed, just cheerfully started again. Sarah smiled at him, thinking that he must be the sweetest-tempered child in the world. He seldom cried—he found everything delightful.

"It's a pity you're not old enough to read," she told him. "You could help me learn my lines."

She acted with the Haven Players, and was rehearsing her role in the latest production, *Laughing All the Way*, a frothy comedy that had been a great hit in the West End of London a few years earlier. It needed a cast of sixteen and three set changes, but no one had ever accused the Haven Players of thinking small.

Sarah was playing Amy, a drab spinster whose life took a new turn after an unexpected avoval of love from Frank, her neighbor. It wasn't the lead, but it was a good part. She enjoyed it, except for having to memorize short lines of dialogue.

"Shakespeare's easier," she confided in Nicky. "Nice long speeches. But these lines are about ten words each, and it's hard to learn them on my own. I need a Frank to rehearse with."

Nicky regarded her sympathetically.

"But I don't have a Frank," Sarah said in an aggrieved voice, "because Mr. James of the dairy got caught by his wife with the woman who sells cosmetics door-to-door. He had to make a fast exit, hotly pursued by the frying pan. I don't know when we'll be seeing him again."

Nicky gurgled agreement and swept his hand across the bricks, sending them tumbling to the floor. Sarah knelt to help him retrieve them. He smiled at her, and she looked into his face with a passion of love. After a moment she heard a man's voice speak somewhere over her head.

"Is anybody here?"

"Sorry, I was just..." Sarah straightened, and the words died on her lips.

"I'm new here," Justin Hallwood said. "I want to buy a map, and maybe you could tell me—hey, are you all right?"

"Yes, I—I'm fine," Sarah managed to say.

"You look as if you've seen a ghost." Justin

grinned. "I'm real enough, and starving. Can you tell me where I can get something to eat?"

Sarah stared at him, trying not to betray her shock. Justin was dressed as she'd never seen him before, in jeans and a checked shirt open at the throat. Over that he wore a casual jacket. There was some stubble on his chin, and his skin was brown, as though he'd spent time in the open air. The Justin Hallwood she'd known had always been expensively and elegantly dressed. This man's shabby comfort was so unlike what she remembered that she wondered if she'd made a mistake.

But only for a moment. There was no other face in the world that could make her heart beat with such wild, painful joy. The firm jaw and straight nose were just as she remembered them. His voice was the voice that had said her name so softly when they held each other in the heat of passion. The generous, sensual mouth was the one she'd kissed a hundred times in reality and a thousand times in her dreams. His deep blue eyes were unchanged.

Except for this. They were empty of all recognition as they looked at her. They were friendly and smiling, but they were the eyes of someone who'd never seen her before in his life. This was the man she had loved, who'd fathered her child. But he didn't know her.

"A place to eat," she echoed abstractedly. "Look, I was just going to make coffee. Why don't you have some with me, and I'll think of somewhere?"

"That sounds nice, if it's no trouble."

Making coffee gave her a chance to collect her scattered wits. Some inkling of the explanation was coming to her. The papers had carried a small item about Justin's accident three months ago, with the mention of head injuries. Sarah had watched fearfully for further news, dreading to hear that he was dead. But there had been nothing more.

Did his appearance here, so unlike his normal self, mean that his mind had been injured, that he no longer knew who he was?

She set coffee and sandwiches before him and tried to speak casually. "Are you taking a vacation, Mr...."

"Hallwood," he said at once. "Justin Hallwood. Please call me Justin. Yes, I'm on a walking tour, enjoying the countryside." He sighed with pleasure. "I'd no idea it was so lovely."

Sarah's mind was whirling. Justin hadn't lost his memory. He just didn't remember her. "It's at its best at this time of year," she said mechanically. "You're not a countryman, then?"

"No, I've always lived in the city, and liked it. But I was in a car smash, and my doctor thought I ought to have a real change before I went back to work. But you haven't told me your name."

"Sarah Conroy," she said slowly, watching him.

He didn't react to her name. He was tucking into the sandwiches like a starving man. Sarah leaned into the playpen and raised Nicky, so that Justin saw him for the first time. "Is he yours?" he asked.

"Yes, he's my son. His name's Nicky."

"Hi, Nicky." The baby gave a shout of pleasure, laughing directly into Justin's face, and he grinned back. "He's a nice little feller. He seems to like me."

Justin waved a finger an inch from Nicky, who seized it in delight.

"Doesn't your employer mind you keeping the baby in the shop?" he asked. "Or is it your shop?"

"My uncle's. The three of us live together in the flat upstairs."

"Just the three of you?"

After a moment she said, "Nicky's father doesn't live with us."

To her astonishment, he reddened. "I'm sorry," he said hastily. "I don't know what made me ask that—it's none of my darned business—please forget it."

"Have some more coffee," she said, taking pity on his confusion. Again she wondered if this could really be Justin Hallwood, a man who'd always said what he pleased and done what he pleased, and to hell with anyone who didn't like it!

"Have you always lived here?" he asked, clearly trying to find a new subject.

"I tried city life for a few years, but it didn't really suit me. I returned to Haven last year when—when I was carrying Nicky. Uncle Nick took me back."

"So you named your son after Uncle Nick?" Justin asked.

"I—yes, yes, I did."

Justin raised an eyebrow at her sudden awkwardness, but Sarah said no more.

Justin finished his snack and said reluctantly, "I suppose I should be moving on."

"Is that wise?" Sarah asked. "You look tired to me. If it was a bad accident perhaps you shouldn't overdo things, especially as you've lost so much—so much strength.''

It was a slip. She'd been going to say ''so much weight.'' Luckily he didn't seem to notice.

''Actually, I do feel a bit done in,'' he admitted. ''I've walked a long way these last couple of days. Does Haven have a good hotel?''

''None, I'm afraid. There's a bed-and-breakfast, but it's very small.''

''I'm not looking for anything grand.'' Justin grinned in self-mockery. ''In fact a grand place probably wouldn't take me, I look so much like a hobo.''

''I really meant that I think they're full at the moment.'' Sarah was talking slowly to give herself time to come to terms with the idea that was forming in her mind. It was madness, and yet...

''We have a spare room upstairs,'' she said, speaking quickly before she lost her courage. ''Uncle Nick and I sometimes take in lodgers. You're welcome to stay here.''

''Are you sure it wouldn't be putting you out?''

''Not at all.''

''There's something you should know before you take me in. I told you I'd had an accident. I had some head injuries and—they affected my mind. I can't remember anything about the last two years. But I'm not dangerous,'' he added quickly. ''It's just that part of me is missing. Some people would be worried by that—''

''I'm not,'' she assured him quickly. So that was the answer. Two years. He really thought they had never met before.

"Are you sure you feel safe?" he persisted. "You know nothing at all about me—"

"Don't worry about it. I know you're not dangerous."

"In that case, thank you." Justin looked up as a large man wearing a police uniform appeared in the doorway.

"Halló," Sarah said with a smile. "This is Justin Hallwood, who's going to be staying with us for a while. Justin, this is Sergeant Reg Mayhew."

The two men greeted each other, and Sarah said, "You're in time for some coffee."

"That's kind of you, but I'm a bit pushed for time," the sergeant said. "Someone's complained about Oppenshaw's dog again, and since I've got to go out there I thought I'd look in and collect the stuff."

"Fine. It's in back, all ready. Uncle Nick will settle up with you when he returns."

"Okay by me. I'll see you, then." He gave a friendly nod to Justin and disappeared into the back of the shop.

"Some of our distant customers need to have things delivered," Sarah explained. "But we can't afford to hire a delivery man. So Reg does it for us whenever he can."

"You mean he delivers your goods in his police car?" Justin asked, grinning.

"That's right. There's not much crime around here, so, as Reg says, he might as well put the car to good use."

Justin rose and began looking around the shop. "I remember a little place like this when I was a child," he said. "It stocked one of everything, because that's all it had room for."

"That's us," Sarah agreed. "It's Uncle Nick's pride that he never lets his customers down, whatever they want—are you all right?"

Justin's face had gone gray suddenly, and Sarah was only just in time to catch him as he swayed. He steadied himself against her, closing his eyes. His brow was damp.

"Sit down," she said, supporting him to the chair. The feel of him in her arms again almost destroyed her composure. Her heart was beating hard, but luckily he was beyond noticing her agitation.

"I guess I overdid it a bit," he said, gasping.

"You certainly have. I don't think you're ready for a walking tour."

"You're probably right. Could I have some water?"

Instead of water she took a bottle of brandy from a shelf and poured him a measure. "Drink this."

He did so, and some color came into his cheeks.

"Perhaps you should lie down," Sarah suggested.

"Thanks, I think I will."

He rose, but closed his eyes immediately. Sarah took his arm and drew it around her shoulders. Together they made their way up the stairs until they reached the spare bedroom. She could see from his eyes that his head was aching badly. "I think I should get the doctor to you," she said worriedly.

"No, no, I'll be fine when I've rested."

She supported him as far as the bed, and he almost fell onto it. His eyes closed immediately and he lay still, as if exhausted. She closed the curtains and drew a cover over him. His face was tense with pain, but gradually it relaxed and his breathing grew regular. She watched him for a moment, thinking of those other times when she'd watched him sleep and wondering what miracle had brought him back to her, the same and yet not the same.

Justin felt as if he was lying at the bottom of the sea. The room in which he awoke was decorated in greenish blue. The curtains had been pulled across the window, but they were thin and only dulled the light. The headache that had come upon him so suddenly was gone, and he felt pleasantly peaceful.

He wasn't sure how long he'd slept, but it had done him good. He felt relaxed and rested, as he hadn't done in the past few weeks. He'd been on edge ever since he awoke from the accident to find that two whole years had vanished from his memory.

At first he'd coped fairly well. The doctor had reassured him that such blank spots were common. His memory would return gradually. But it hadn't. Justin had insisted on going back to work, only to find that he was useless because his own deals were strange to him. And not only strange, but displeasing. The documents revealed a ruthlessness that filled him with dismay, and he'd immediately reversed some of his own decisions. Greg had been delighted to see Foster's reprieved but had torn his hair at the chaos Justin's change of mind caused.

Marguerite was another problem. When she'd appeared by his bed, mourning the postponement of their wedding plans, he'd felt a sense of horror. How had

he ever suggested marriage to this chilly, glittery creature? And how was he to get out of it?

Greg had come to his rescue. "You're not engaged
to her, no matter what she says," he told his relieved
brother. "We all thought you were going to propose
at her birthday party. So did she, but you gave her that
car instead. She wasn't pleased."

He'd been relieved to know the truth but disturbed
that he'd apparently been on the verge of committing
himself to such a woman. He'd begun to worry about
the man he'd been during the past two years.

He tried to force his mind to remember. He had
brain scans and psychiatric tests, and the doctors reassured him that he was completely normal—except
that he'd lost two years.

His last recollection was the day before the Carter
Vernon reception to celebrate his victory over a
smaller firm that had had the temerity to stand up to
him. He'd studied the guest list and discovered that
Marguerite had come with Jack Vernon. But when
he'd asked her about him she'd been dismissive.

"Oh, darling, forget him. He was nothing. It was
wonderful how you just crushed him and took what
you wanted. I do so admire that in a man."

And I? he wondered. *Was that what I thought of as
admirable behavior?*

He had more tests, experimenting with verbal as-
sociation in the hope that some word or phrase would
trigger his memory. But he'd only become tense and
exhausted with strain.

"That's enough," his doctor said at last. "You
can't force it, and you'll only make things worse by

trying. You want my prescription? Get out of here.
Leave London, and put the firm behind you. Have a
good time."

"A good time?" he echoed, as if the words were
in a foreign language. As far as he could recall his
vacations had always been business opportunities—a
week spent on a customer's yacht, a skiing trip in one
of those snowy playgrounds where money congre-
gated. Pleasure had never been part of it.

"How can I have a good time with this weighing
on my mind?" he growled.

The elderly doctor had looked at him shrewdly.
"That's the medicine," he said. "Forget yourself.
Then maybe you'll find yourself."

Justin had handed the reins of the firm to his brother
and driven away with no clear idea where he was going. He'd found himself traveling through green countryside on his way to the next town. But he'd never
reached the town. He'd stopped at a small pub that
took paying guests and rented a room. He spent the
next day wandering through meadows and woods, enjoying the peace that had never meant anything to him
before. He had bought a large-scale map of the local-
ity.

The landlord told him that most of the places were
so small only the bigger maps mentioned them. He ran
over the names until he came to Haven. It was about
a hundred miles away, near the sea. It would make a
handy focus for his journey.

"It's not much of a place," the landlord said.
"Nothing special to go there for."

"There's the sea," Justin objected.

"If you want the sea you'll do better a few miles further along."

"No," Justin said stubbornly. "Haven."

He garaged the car and bought a pair of sturdy boots. On the first day he walked too far, but he had a sense of being driven to reach his destination without delay. He stayed overnight in a tiny village, and in the local craft shop he discovered a man carving things from wood. Impulsively Justin demanded to be taught. He had the hands of an engineer, half artist, half workman, with long, powerful fingers. He'd always loved working with his hands, but he'd given it up long ago, in favor of making money. Now the old pleasure returned, and with it the sensation of recovering a part of himself. After a few hours' work he had a tall staff that was just the thing to support his aching frame on the journey.

He lingered, talking to Martin, the shop's owner, who invited him to supper. He had a sturdy wife and a grave, studious little girl of nine, called Katie, who was fascinated by the sight of Justin with the staff. "You look like the hero of the *Pilgrim's Progress*," she said. "I've been reading it."

She showed him the book with its illustration of a traveler plodding on his way, staff in hand. "Are you going to the Celestial City?" she asked.

"No, just to Haven."

"Is Haven a very nice place?"

"I don't know. I've never been there."

"Are you going to visit someone who lives there?"

"No, I..." The words trailed away as he had a

strange dizzy feeling. He'd walked too strenuously that day. "No."

"Then why are you going?" she demanded reasonably.

He felt suddenly disoriented. He didn't know why he was going to Haven, only that he had to. He tried to answer, but no words would come.

Martin came to his rescue. "Leave the poor fellow in peace, Katie, and sit at the table."

She obeyed her father, saying, "I thought you might be going on a pilgrimage. Haven means refuge or sanctuary, doesn't it? So it would be a good place for a pilgrimage."

Her words had stayed with him. Of course his journey wasn't a pilgrimage, yet it was strange how the idea of this one place had taken hold of him so that he was impatient to get there.

On the last lap he'd walked too far in one go, trying to make it before dark. He'd failed and been forced to sleep in a town three miles away. His body ached, but he'd been up early next day, skipping breakfast, eager to get started. And he'd paid the penalty, collapsing almost as soon as he arrived.

The face of Sarah Conroy floated into his consciousness, and he experienced again the half-painful delight he'd felt when he first saw her. Every line of her was still clear—the worn jeans, the blue shirt roped in at her waist with a man's tie, the white column of her throat and above it the gentle, smiling face. Her brown hair had been inexpertly pinned up, and as she talked she seized stray tendrils and put them back, but they soon escaped again. She was natural and unsophisticated, in contrast to what he had appreciated in women—up to two years ago.

But it was her eyes that moved him. They were dark and glowed softly against her warm skin. They'd held an odd, arrested look at the sight of him and he'd wondered if he looked more like a tramp than he knew.

Then her smile had come, breathtaking and beautiful, making him want to stay and go on looking at her. The sight of her son, with the suggestion of a man in her life, had given him a twinge of dismay. His glance had flashed to her left hand. No ring—that was good. When she'd said that Nicky's father wasn't around he'd felt irrational relief.

He'd felt compelled to admit his memory loss, although he feared the effect it might have on her. The gap in his mind made him feel like a freak. The relief when she shrugged it aside had been overwhelming.

He glanced at his watch and was astonished to find it was nearly six in the evening. He'd slept for six hours. He went downstairs to find her just ready to close the shop. "Do you have a map of Haven?" he asked.

She produced one from a high shelf, and he bought it.

"The last sale of the day," Sarah said as she put the money in the till.

She locked the front door, but as she reached up to the top to slide home a bolt a young man with a girlishly good-looking face appeared outside and began asking, through the glass, for her to reopen. "Not a chance," Sarah called to him. "It's five past six."

The boy put his hands together in a pleading gesture.

"No," she called firmly. "Learn to get here on time."

He went into a theatrical pantomime of despair, then pointed a finger at his own heart as if about to shoot himself.

"Oh, all right," Sarah said, laughing. She unlocked the door. "This is positively the last time I do this, Alex."

"You always say that," he said winningly. "But you can't resist me, can you?"

"Very easily," she declared, but she was smiling indulgently. "Hurry up, I want to close."

The young man lingered for a few minutes, flirting with Sarah, before buying a box of chocolates. "For my mother," he said. "To cheer her up."

"To get back in her good books, you mean," Sarah said. "There are no secrets in this place."

"Darling, whatever you've heard, don't believe it." He blew her a kiss and departed with an appraising glance at Justin.

"Let me lock up," Justin said quickly. "I can reach that high bolt more easily than you." He turned the key and slammed the bolt home. When he saw the young man looking back at the shop he pulled down the blind firmly.

"Can I help you with anything?" he asked.

Sarah had lifted her son. "You could carry his playpen, thank you," she said.

Upstairs she indicated the living room and asked him to set the pen there. "Right in the line of the door," she said. "Then I can keep an eye on him while I start supper."

"Leave him to me," Justin said, taking Nicky from her arms.

He followed her into the small, immaculate kitchen, sat on a chair by the wall and settled Nicky between his feet with a toy. "Who's the young man who thinks the world must bow to his convenience?" he asked casually.

"Alex Drew," Sarah said, lighting the gas stove. "He lives in Haven Manor, the big house on the other side of the crossroads. His parents are well off, and I suppose he *is* a bit spoiled. He doesn't seem able to hold down a job, but he's so charming that people forgive him."

"And he trades on it," Justin said wryly.

"Oh, he's all right. He's young."

Justin was about to say something else when he became aware that Nicky was tugging on his wrist. Looking down, he realized that the child was hauling himself to his feet. Justin grinned and helped him up. "How old is your son?"

"Fifteen months. He's already taken his first step," Sarah said proudly. "The doctor says he's advanced."

Nicky slid to the floor but immediately began to haul himself up again. Justin tensed his arm to give the child a lever. Nicky was scowling with concentration, but the scowl turned into a grin when he'd achieved his goal.

"Now, young man, time for bath and bed," Sarah said. "Could you watch the pots for me while I'm away?'' She scooped Nicky up and carried him to the bathroom.

Justin studied the map he had bought. It showed that Haven was built around a set of crossroads. One corner was taken up by Mottson's General Store, standing next to the local tavern, the Haystack. On the next corner was Haven Manor. Justin could see it through the kitchen window. It was obviously the largest and wealthiest house in the village. The church stood on the corner across the way. It was a small, pretty building, surrounded by trees.

The crossroads were uneven, and the fourth corner was much larger than the others. On this corner was an area of grass that stretched out of sight. Nearest to Justin was a pond, with several contented-looking ducks.

A hiss from the gas stove brought Justin to his surroundings, not quite in time to stop the potatoes boiling over. Cursing roundly, he turned the gas off and hastily checked the other pans. But they were behaving themselves.

''Everything all right?'' Sarah called.

''Fine,'' he lied, frantically relighting the gas. Her chuckle floated out to him, and he had the feeling she knew just what had happened. After a moment he grinned at himself. ''Perhaps you'd better take a look,'' he called.

''Can you keep an eye on Nicky?''

He went into the bathroom. The little bath was a quarter filled with water on which floated all manner of animals. Nicky was sitting at one end promoting a race between a duck and an alligator by agitating the water. "Just watch him to make sure he doesn't slide under," Sarah said, rushing out in response to more explosive noises from the kitchen.

The duck and alligator had reached the line. Justin put them back to the start. "We could add the whale, too," he suggested. "What do you think?"

Nicky considered the animals, then looked up and considered Justin. Without warning he raised both hands and brought them down with all his strength. Water flew up and descended, leaving Justin drenched. His indignant cry was drowned by Nicky's yells of delight.

Justin groped blindly for a towel and managed to clear his eyes and mop his hair just in time for Nicky to do it all again. A choke from the doorway made him turn his head. Through his streaming eyes he managed to see Sarah trying to control her laughter.

"That's his favorite trick just now," she said. "He loves water. I'm sorry, I should have warned you."

"Don't mention it," he said, dabbing at himself with the towel. "I think I'll go and find a dry shirt."

When he went into the living room Nicky was sitting in his high chair while his mother spooned puree into his mouth. At least, she aimed for his mouth, but a fair amount ended up on his cheeks and his bib. A delicious smell was coming from the kitchen.

Justin looked around the room, which seemed to have been furnished with antiques. Sketches of flowers adorned the walls, and the whole atmosphere was of a slightly shabby coziness.

"Is that enough?" Sarah asked Nicky. "Right, then, time for bed. Your eyes are drooping." She lifted him out of the high chair. "Come on, my little man," she whispered.

The child was already half-asleep against her shoulder. Justin saw her bury her face against him before carrying him gently away.

They had supper on a table made of dark mahogany in an elegant eighteenth-century design. Justin commented on the number of antiques in the room. "They're not antiques, I'm afraid," Sarah said ruefully. "Poor Uncle Nick lives for the day when he'll find a real treasure, but so far all he's brought home are fakes. This table was supposed to be Chippendale, but it's an imitation."

"They're lovely pieces, anyway."

"That's what I say. But Uncle Nick will never be content until he finds the real thing. Just once, that's all he asks. That's where he's gone today, to an auction in the hope of striking it lucky."

He tucked into the meal like a man who hadn't eaten for days. Sarah watched him, trying to come to terms with the miracle that had brought into the shop the man she'd thought never to see again. Since the day she'd fled his apartment after uttering terrible words, she'd allowed herself to love only her uncle and her son. Her love for Justin was not dead but shut away, hidden where it could no longer hurt her.

But in the first moment of seeing him she'd known that nothing had changed. Her feelings had survived, as intense, anguished and joyful as they had ever been. She loved him still. She would always love him.

But he had altered. In the past he'd seldom relaxed over a meal. There'd been a phone call to make or listen for, a strategy to plan. Now he seemed content to be where he was. When he held out his plate for more with a rueful grin, her happiness bubbled up like a wellspring.

She refused his offer to help with the washing up and encouraged him to go to bed early. Despite his sleep that afternoon she could sense that he wasn't yet fully rested.

She had an early night herself and quickly fell into a contented doze. But after a couple of hours she awoke with a fearful conviction that it had all been a dream. She crept out of bed and along the corridor to his room, walking carefully, for the floor was uneven and the boards creaked. To her relief she could hear him breathing. The door was slightly ajar, and she risked nudging it open a little and looking in.

He lay in a shaft of moonlight. Nervous, yet unable to stop herself, she slipped in and knelt beside him, her face only a few inches from his. She was free to look with longing. Sometimes in the past she'd seen him like this, but not often. He didn't like to be observed when he was asleep. He hadn't said why, but she guessed it made him feel vulnerable. It had hurt that he didn't trust her enough to relax.

Now she felt like a thief, stealing her joy from a defenseless man, but she couldn't help it. After the long, lonely months, nothing could have stopped her from taking this moment. Perhaps it was all she would have.

"I love you," she whispered. "I never stopped loving you. I never will."

He stirred, and she rose quickly and fled. In her

room Nicky had just awakened. She scooped him up and held him tightly to her.

"He's come back to us, my darling," she whispered. "Do you hear that? He's come back to us."

Chapter Three

"Tell me about Haven," Justin said over breakfast next morning. "How big is it?"

"About eight hundred people."

He was startled. He'd addressed conference halls containing more people than that. "It won't take me long to explore, then," he said, consulting his map. "I'll go down the High Street, Fennicott Lane—"

"Then you'll pass Miss Timmins's house. Could you let her know that I've got the special cat food she wanted?"

"I'll take it, if you like."

"Are you sure? I've no right to make a delivery man of you—"

"It's fine. I may as well be useful. Why is it special cat food?"

"It's an expensive line that I wouldn't otherwise

carry, but nothing's too good for Crosspatch. He's Miss Timmins's only companion, and I think she goes short of food herself to give him the best.''

He went out half an hour later, bearing six tins of cat food. ''Tell her to drop in and pay for them whenever she can spare the time,'' Sarah said. ''Her pension's not due until Friday, so she won't be able to afford them until then, but don't let on you know that.''

Justin started his exploration with Haven Manor, the home of Alex Drew, to whom he'd taken an unaccountable dislike. It was exactly the kind of house he would have expected to produce such a thoughtless young puppy. The manor was in the heart of the village yet managed to be apart from it. The large house stood well back from the road, protected by high walls and wrought-iron gates. Through the gates Justin could see a good deal of the life of the Drew family.

Two luxury cars were parked in the driveway. To one side of the house was a set of stables. Two Thoroughbred horses were just being led out by a groom, and the next moment Alex Drew appeared, dressed for riding. With him was a middle-aged woman with a hard face who looked just enough like him to be his mother.

They swung themselves into the saddles, and the groom ran to pull open the gates. Alex gave him a cheeky grin as he rode past, but the woman started straight ahead, ignoring Justin's presence. The groom blew out his cheeks in relief. ''She's in a bad mood today,'' he confided.

"She looks as if she was often in a bad mood," Justin said.

"A real Tartar. It's him, her son. Home again. Another job gone down the drain 'cause the boss caught him fiddling the cash. He's useless." He glanced over Justin's shoulder, and alarm overtook his face. Turning, Justin saw that Mrs. Drew had looked back and was frowning.

"Oh, gawd, she'll have my hide for gossiping," the groom moaned. He shut the gate and fled.

Miss Timmins was in her garden, weeding energetically. She was a tiny, birdlike woman who regarded Justin quizzically until he mentioned Sarah's name and presented the tins.

"How very kind of you. I was just about to have some tea. Do come and join me."

He stepped into the tiny cottage, bending his head to avoid the low beams. It was spotless and smelled deliciously of furniture polish, but Justin, born in poverty, could recognize the telltale signs of a small income stretched to the limit. Miss Timmins was making a great show of hunting for her purse, much as he'd once seen his own mother do.

"I'm not authorized to take money," he explained quickly. "Sarah says you can drop in to pay when you've got a moment?"

"How kind of her. I shall be rather busy until Friday—"

"Friday will do fine."

While they were drinking tea the cat appeared. From the price of the food Justin had expected a pedigree Persian at the least, but Crosspatch was an angular

black tom. A hundred fights had left his ears so torn
they appeared to be fringed, but he had a certain mag-
nificence as he regarded the newcomer with lofty dis-
dain.

"Home at last, my pet," Miss Timmins called, add-
ing with unexpected robustness, "been out on the tiles
again?"

"Does he do that often?" Justin asked, grinning.

"Most nights, especially at this time of year," Miss
Timmins said seriously. "I'm always afraid he won't
come back."

"Couldn't you have him, er..."

"Oh, I couldn't do that. Spoil his fun. One should
have a sense of the *fitness* of things, don't you think?"

"Absolutely," Justin said.

"I got him nine years ago. Since then the number
of black kittens in this area has gone right up." She
added conspiratorially, "Mrs. Drew hates him, you
know. She breeds pedigree Siamese, and their quarters
are like an armed camp. If he's late back, I always
worry in case she's done something wicked to him."

Further exploration revealed to Justin that Haven
was barely provided with necessary shops. There was
no butcher. Sarah stocked some frozen meat, and anyone who wanted fresh drove to the little town of Market Dorsey, six miles away. Prescription medicines
had to be bought there, too. Aspirin and bandages
could be obtained in the tiny newsagent that doubled
as a post office.

So Justin was surprised to discover a well-stocked
antique shop. He knew just enough about antiques to
recognize a few really valuable pieces and wondered

where Colly Davids, the elderly owner, found his trade in this sleepy place.

He got his answer over a cup of coffee, which the hospitable Colly pressed on him. "I don't sell to Haven," he confided. "Few people here could afford my prices. Besides, none of them know the real from the fake, although that old fool, Nick Mottson, thinks he does. I buy and sell internationally. I've got my own newsletter."

He produced a copy, and Justin commented on the professional production.

"My granddaughter, Brenda, does desktop publishing on her computer," Colly explained. "She produces this for me in between writing for the local paper, and we send it all over the world. Of course, not all my customers need it. Some of them just visit our web site." He saw the look of surprise Justin wasn't quick enough to hide and added mischievously, "We're quite civilized out here, you know. Some of us can even read and write."

"I'm sorry," Justin said, reddening. "I didn't mean—"

"Oh, we're used to being thought of as a load of hayseeds. Now, if you're going past the pub I wonder if you'd give a few copies to Ted, the landlord. He likes to have them lying about. It doesn't bring me any business, of course, but he feels it gives the Haystack a touch of class, and I don't mind doing him a kindness."

By now Justin was getting the feel of the village, so it was no surprise when Ted received the newsletters with the cheery words, "It helps Colly's business if people can see his stuff when they drop in for a drink. I sometimes wonder how he'd manage without my help. But there! I don't mind doing him a kindness."

On learning where he was staying, Ted scribbled a list for him to give to Sarah. "It's my usual order, with a few things extra," he said. "If you wouldn't mind…"

"No problem," Justin said, pocketing the list.

At the far side of the village green stood a building that could only be described as a mishmash. Parts of it were weather-beaten stone, parts were brick. At one end stood a stone bell tower, giving the building the look of a church, an impression that was strengthened by the gargoyles flaring out over the green. Justin studied the ugly carved faces, fascinated.

"It's a bit of a monstrosity, isn't it?"

Justin turned and found a middle-aged vicar with a thin, amiable face. "How do you do?" the vicar said. "My name's George Frensham, and I know you're Sarah's lodger."

"News travels fast."

"No secrets in a small place like this."

"It looks like a church," Justin said, "but surely that's the church over there?" He pointed to a gray building that could just be seen between trees.

"This was once the village church," Reverend Frensham explained. "It was built six hundred years ago, but it caught fire in the last century. They patched it up as best they could, which wasn't very well, as you can see. But in the end they built a new church and abandoned this one. Now we use it as a community hall. It's drafty and inconvenient, but it's got masses of character, and we're fond of it."

He led the way to the tower. The old door was locked. George took the key from his pocket and showed Justin in. "Strictly speaking, nobody's allowed in here, for safety reasons," he said. "But every month I pop in to check the place."

High up in the gloom the huge bell seemed to menace them silently.

"He's called Great Gavin," the vicar said. "The timbers up there are in a bad way, so I suppose we should take him down, but he's been a good friend to Haven. For centuries he was used to warn the village of flood or fire. It would seem a poor return to simply throw him away."

As they came into the sunlight Justin could hear the sound of a piano and a woman's voice calling, "Bend and stretch—bend and stretch—*stretch*, Mrs. Adams. No cheating now."

"The hall's kept pretty busy?" he asked, noticing a board with a rota.

"Oh, there's always something. The exercise class, the gardening club, the campaign for traditional beer—although they usually prefer to meet in the pub—the amateur dramatic society—"

"You put on plays, too, in this little place?"

"Plays and musicals," the vicar said cheerfully. "Of course, the piano is a little out of tune, as you can hear, otherwise we were thinking of doing *Carousel* this year."

Justin stared, speechless.

He was swept off for tea at the vicarage and shown

the vegetables George grew in every available corner
of the large vicarage grounds. He left with a written
order for Sarah and the news that George would bring
her some vegetables for the shop the following day.

As soon as he turned into the main road he found
himself confronting a flock of sheep, and in a moment
they surrounded him. A buxom young woman was
chivvying them along, and she waved to him in greeting. "Milking time," she said cheerfully.

He was too astonished to speak. He stood there
while the flock swirled around him and passed on,
leaving him in the road.

He walked for another few minutes before realizing
that he'd left the village. Turning, he went back and
explored the side roads, but in half an hour he was out
of Haven again. Around him stretched fields in which
cattle grazed, and in the distance he could see a farmhouse.

He leaned against a fence, feeling oddly disappointed. Was that it? All of it? Haven was charming,
of course, and the peace and quiet were pleasant after
his recent experiences. But he couldn't imagine staying here for more than a couple of days without becoming bored. Despite his lost years he knew the man
he'd been before that—ambitious, driving, hard-
headed, seeking power through size, determined that
Hallwood Construction and Engineering would dominate the market. He was still that man.

But his disappointment had a deeper cause, one he
was reluctant to face because it was irrational, and he
was a rational man. It had to do with the sense of
pilgrimage that had come over him on the road. For a

while Haven had seemed like a sanctuary, beckoning him on. Now here it was, a place the size of a postage stamp, where the big news of the day was that Crosspatch had been pursuing Mrs. Drew's Siamese, life moved at a sheep's pace, and nobody seemed to have heard of the telephone. He thought of his headquarters, where big decisions were made. What would these people know of the real world?

Suddenly he felt foolish, and that passed easily into irritation. As he made his way back he was determined to tell Sarah he would be leaving the next day. It was time to return to work, take a hold of himself and force his memory to do his will.

He found the shop shut, for it was early closing. Letting himself in at the side, he was assailed by the delicious smell of home cooking. Sarah was in the kitchen, up to her elbows in flour. She wore a yellow dress, the color accentuated by the sunlight streaming in through the window. At her feet Nicky was tearing up paper and clamoring for her attention. She gave it, laughing, kissed him and went back to her work. Justin stood unnoticed, feeling inexplicable happiness steal over him. His irritation seemed to be draining away out of the soles of his feet.

It was Nicky who noticed and gave a shout of glee. Sarah looked up, smiling. Meeting her eyes, Justin had the same sensation he'd known at their meeting the day before, a delight that was almost painful in its intensity.

"Could you put the kettle on for me?" Sarah asked, waving her floury arms.

He did so, observing, "I shall be afloat at this rate.

I had coffee with Colly Davids, who spoke slightingly about your uncle's knowledge of antiques—''

Sarah chuckled. ''Did he call him an old fool?''

'''Fraid so.''

''That's nothing to what Uncle Nick calls him. They have a deadly feud, which they both enjoy enormously.''

Justin grinned. ''I thought it might be something like that. I also had two cups of tea with the vicar, plus one of the best rock cakes I've ever tasted. He'll bring you some vegetables tomorrow.''

''Oh, good. His stuff is wonderful. I get queues down the street for his asparagus.''

''Is the vicar allowed to use the vicarage for a commercial undertaking?'' Justin asked with a grin.

''Probably not,'' Sarah observed serenely. ''But he needs the money. He's a demon plumber, too—mended our cistern last year.''

Justin began to laugh. Sarah watched him with a pleasure that was partly relief. Yesterday he'd returned to her out of the void by a process that almost seemed magic. When he'd strode out this morning she'd half expected him to disappear into the void again.

Yet here he was, relaxed and genial. Her heart overflowed with happiness, and she had to struggle not to let her gaze rest on him too often in case he read her feelings. Once she risked a quick glance, only to find him watching her with a strange smile on his face. She looked away, but she could feel the tide of color sweep into her cheeks.

''I took the chance to do a batch of cooking,'' she

said, for something to say. "You need feeding up. You're much too thin."

"That's the result of the accident," he said. "But Sarah, I was going to say, about my staying here—"

She raised her head. Her cheeks were prettily flushed, and there was a dab of flour on the end of her nose. Suddenly Justin found that his speech about departure wouldn't get itself said.

"What was it, Justin?"

"Well—we didn't talk about how much I was to pay you. It's not just the room—you're cooking for me, as well. How about...?" He named a figure, and Sarah's eyebrows rose.

"I can't take all that," she said, scandalized. "It's far too much."

"As long as it's not too little. Right, that's settled." He would stay until the end of the week.

"Before I forget," he said, reaching into his pocket, "I've written down various messages for you." She studied them, thanked him and pinned them up. "I don't mind," he said, "but why don't they just telephone?"

"They probably would have if you hadn't happened by. But why use a phone when there are people?"

"No reason, I guess. By the way, I think my hearing must be failing. I was ambushed by a gang of sheep. The woman with them said something about *milking* time, but I couldn't have heard that right."

"Oh, yes, sheep milk makes lovely cheese. They belong to Penny Farm, just outside the village. The farmer grazes some of his flock in the churchyard, so he gets the grass and the vicar doesn't have to pay anyone to cut it. He takes the sheep home at milking time and returns them afterward. The quickest way is through the village.''

''What do passing motorists do?''

''They wait.''

Justin grinned. ''I should have thought of that.''

Sarah was just making the supper and about to call Justin when a shape darkened the doorway. ''Uncle Nick,'' she cried eagerly, giving him a bear hug. He was a large, heavily built man, with a gray beard and a head of white hair. He hugged her, then did a little jig as nimbly as his bulk would allow.

''I did it,'' he carolled. ''I finally did it.''

''You got a real antique?'' she asked breathlessly.

''A Hepplewhite cabinet in good condition, and it only cost me sixty pounds.''

''The owner let it go for that?''

''Oh, he didn't know what he had, but you can't fool me.'' Sarah forbore to mention the number of times he'd been fooled. ''That cabinet is genuine eighteenth century, made by George Hepplewhite, or I'm a Dutchman. Now, what's been happening while I was gone?''

''We've got a lodger. His name's Justin Hallwood, and he walked in here yesterday morning and collapsed—because he was in a car crash—and he's taking a walking holiday because he was badly hurt.'' Sarah gabbled the words slightly, hoping her self-consciousness didn't show.

The old man was still. He seemed struck by a thought.

"Uncle Nick?"

"Sorry, darling. That was a bit jumbled, and I was trying to sort it out. Are you sure this isn't too much work for you?"

"No, he's being a real help. That sounds like him now."

Uncle Nick turned to look at the tall man who appeared in the doorway. "Sarah's been telling me about you," he said, holding out his hand.

They shook and uttered courtesies. Justin could see that Uncle Nick was sizing him up, which was disconcerting. He was usually the one doing the sizing. He seemed to pass, however, for Nick grunted and turned his attention to food.

Over supper he questioned Justin, politely but insistently. "Sarah says you had an accident."

"That's right. It's taken the last two years out of my life."

"You mean you can't remember?" Uncle Nick asked with a touch of sharpness.

"That's right."

"What, *nothing?*"

"Uncle Nick," Sarah protested.

"All right, all right. At my age a man's allowed to forget his manners occasionally. Don't mind my asking, do you?" he demanded.

"Not at all," Justin assured him, although the subject made him uncomfortable.

"Well, I mind," Sarah said firmly. "I want to hear some more about your Hepplewhite cabinet."

Luckily this distracted Nick. "Ha!" he said gleefully. "You wait until Colly sees it. He'll be green with envy. Now, don't make that face, Sarah. I know you mean well, but you don't know anything about antiques.''

"Neither do you, according to Colly Davids," Justin said with a grin.

"Colly Davids is a stubborn, pigheaded bigot," Uncle Nick growled. "And if you've been listening to him you've been wasting your time."

"When do we see this cabinet?" Sarah asked.

"Soon. I'll have to borrow Ted's van to fetch it."

Soon after supper Justin yawned and said he was going to bed. He wanted to call Greg on his mobile phone, and he thought Sarah would like to be alone with her uncle. Besides, the curious looks Nick was giving him were beginning to make him uneasy.

For a long time after he'd gone Uncle Nick was sunk in thought. A heaviness seemed to have settled over him. At last he said, "So that's him."

"Pardon?"

"Darling, I'm not a fool. That's Nicky's father."

"Shh!" she said urgently and went to the door. But the corridor outside was empty. "I don't know why you should say that—"

"Because his name's Justin, which is Nicky's first name, too. Because his eyes are the same. And because you light up for him, which is strange if you only met him yesterday. But you didn't, did you? You met him two years ago."

Sarah dropped on her knees beside his chair and spoke urgently. "Uncle Nick, you've got to promise not to say a word. He doesn't know. He told you what's happened to his memory. *He* thinks we only met yesterday, and I want to keep it that way for a while. It wouldn't help to tell him if he can't remember. He might think I was making it up and go away.''

''And would that be so terrible?'' he asked gently.

''Yes,'' she said huskily. ''Yes, it would.''

He stroked her face. ''He hurt you so much once. I don't want to see him hurt you again.''

''But he's so different now.''

''And how long will that last?''

She shook her head mutely, for it was the question she asked herself all the time.

''Isn't he really the same hard man underneath?'' Uncle Nick persisted.

''I don't know,'' she sighed. ''I hope not.''

''People don't change, love.''

''They can,'' she said passionately. ''Sometimes they can. Promise me that you'll say nothing.''

''All right, darling. You must do this your way. But please be careful.''

Next day Ted readily agreed to lend his van. Uncle Nick announced that he was too tired to make the journey again.

''You do it,'' he said to Sarah. ''Justin, why don't you go along and see a bit of the country hereabouts?''

So it was settled, and Justin, Sarah and the baby piled into the van to set off for Stanways, the great country house whose contents had been sold at auction. As they were about to start up Colly appeared, on his way to buy some tea. ''Are you off to Stanways?'' he called.

Sarah leaned out. "Yes, we're going to fetch something for Uncle Nick," she said guardedly.

"Ah, yes. I heard he was at the sale. I looked the house over last year. Nothing of interest. There was a cabinet they were trying to pass off as Hepplewhite. Good fake, but I expect Nick saw through it. Bye!" He went into the shop, chuckling.

"Oh, dear!" Sarah said.

Justin drove the first part of the way. They stopped at a café on the coast and drank coffee looking out at the glittering sea. "Why do you keep flexing your hand like that?" Sarah asked.

"It's a long time since I've driven a vehicle so—so..."

"Prehistoric?" she asked mischievously.

"Thank you, yes. I suppose I might have driven one in the last two years, but I somehow doubt it."

"No, you—" Sarah checked herself hastily. She'd been about to say something about his sleek, gleaming car, forgetting that he didn't know she'd ever seen it. "You've probably never even seen one so old," she amended hastily.

In fact Justin had said nothing that might connect him with the wealth and power that were his. His clothes were casual, and he'd removed his expensive watch, replacing it with one he'd bought at the newsagent for less than ten pounds. Some deep instinct he hadn't analyzed had told him to approach this new situation without baggage from the past.

When they restarted the journey Sarah took the wheel. "I've driven this thing before, and I've got the muscles to prove it," she said with a laugh. "You don't mind sitting with Nick, do you?"

The child was strapped into his safety seat at the back, and Justin took his place next to it. He talked to Nicky in a soft voice for the rest of the journey. Sarah couldn't make out much, but now and then she heard Nicky's voice raised in a gurgle of laughter. Justin seemed to be explaining something seriously, not talking down, but treating Nicky in a man-to-man fashion that they obviously both found pleasant. She smiled to herself.

They reached Stanways in the early afternoon. It was a magnificent house that had fallen on hard times. All the furniture had been auctioned off, and several other collection vans were already in place. They were taken inside to see the cabinet, which was certainly a beautiful piece with an elegant design and a satin finish. A workman helped Justin carry it outside and load it into the van. He lashed it into place with ropes, and they were ready for the return journey.

"I'm starving," Justin announced at last. "Let me buy you a good lunch."

"But I've brought things for a picnic," she said. "You can't eat indoors on a day like this."

They found a sheltered spot by a stream. Sarah took a thick blanket from the back of the truck and spread it on the ground under a tree. Justin unpacked the basket, listing the contents as he did so.

"Chicken salad, rolls, pâté, wine, coffee—you thought of everything."

He buttered the rolls while Sarah fed Nicky. A deep, physical contentment pervaded her. It was bliss to sit there, drinking wine, watching the sun slanting through the branches and listening to the soft bubble of the water over stones. But the greatest happiness was to share these things with Justin and know that he, too, was enjoying what he would once have despised.

"Do you think Colly's right about that cabinet?" Justin asked after a while. "It looks a wonderful piece to me."

"I think it's lovely, too, but Colly knows his subject. If he's given the thumbs-down, I'm afraid that's it. Poor Uncle Nick. He'll be so disappointed."

"Why does it mean so much to him? Is he trying to make his fortune?"

"Oh, no, it's not the money. If he ever finds the real thing he won't sell it, he'll treasure it as proof that his philosophy of life was right, after all."

"What's his philosophy?"

"That no matter how bad life seems there's always hidden beauty, if you look for it. I remember him saying things like that all through my childhood. Uncle Nick's lost so many people. He was close to his brother, my mother's father, but he and his wife were killed in a car crash, so Uncle Nick took my mother in and treated her like a daughter. He loved her so much. He said she was the touch of beauty that made the tragedy bearable.

"My father went away when I was a child, and there was a divorce. Uncle Nick just said that we'd always have a home with him. And when Mom died four years ago, he said to me, 'Nothing can be really bad as long as I have you.' I broke his heart when I left because I wanted a more exciting life. But when I came home carrying Nicky, he just welcomed me without question. And he adores Nicky. He's the touch of beauty now, the good that came out of bad. For me, too. Uncle Nick's philosophy is catching.''

"And did it help you survive the bad?" Justin asked quietly.

"Oh, yes. I knew I had my miracle, and it would make everything worthwhile. I could never wish Nicky unborn. I only wish—''

She stopped. She'd been carried away by what she was saying and had almost forgotten who she was talking to. For a moment she'd hovered on the verge of saying she wished Nicky's father could have shared the joy. Justin was looking at her with grave eyes.

"What do you wish?" he asked. "That *he* was here with you now?"

A flash of recklessness made her say, "He *is* here. He'll never be far away from me.''

"Because you have his son?"

"Yes—and my memories.''

"Ah, yes, memories," he said with a touch of bitterness. "You don't know how valuable they are until you lose them.''

"Justin, I'm sorry. That was stupid and careless of me.''

"Don't apologize. Why should you guard your tongue because I'm a freak?"

"You're not a freak," she protested warmly.

"Aren't I? I feel like one to myself. I watched your face as you were talking. It was full of memories, happy ones and sad ones, but even the worst of them made up part of an experience that went to create you."

"But you haven't forgotten everything."

"No, but I need to know what I was doing last year, and the year before. I can't work because I can't recognize my own decisions or my own thinking. Some of the things I did seem so bizarre to me I can't believe it was me. I'm like a man who came back from the dead. I know my name, but *I don't know who I am.*"

He finished on a cry of pain. The underlying tension that ruled his life these days had broken free, and he couldn't control the feelings of desperation. But the next moment he forced himself to smile.

"Sorry about that. I've got no right to dump all this on you. It's just that I find you so easy to talk to. After two days it's like I've known you all my life. You don't think I'm crazy, do you?"

"No," she said tenderly. "I don't think you're crazy. I want you to talk to me. I want you to tell me everything."

"You'd find it pretty weird."

"Try me."

Justin ran his hand through his hair. "I hate being confused," he said somberly, "especially about myself. The doctors said it would start coming back bit by bit, but—nothing. Just a solid block of emptiness. *Why?* Why those two years? Why not two months? Or five years? Or ten? Why have I blotted out that time and no other?

"I feel as if it's all there, waiting for me, just around a corner. I only have to turn that corner, but whenever I try there's something I can't get past."

"Isn't there anyone who can tell you what you need to know?"

"Sure. My brother's told me a lot, but—in some ways that's the worst thing, when someone tells you and you *still* can't remember. It sounds ungrateful, but you end up wishing they hadn't said anything. And sometimes—people make it worse by pursuing their own agenda, claiming things that aren't true, counting on you not knowing the difference." He was thinking of Marguerite, but he didn't want to introduce her name into the magical atmosphere developing between himself and Sarah.

Sarah blessed the instinct that had made her keep quiet. How much damage she might have caused by unloading the story onto a man who'd grown suspicious! "What's the last thing you remember?" she asked cautiously.

"It was a day when nothing special happened. That's the strange part. Everything was the same, except that the work was a little rushed because there was a big reception that day. I'd taken over a firm called Carter Vernon, and I was marking the merger with a shindig at Jaquino's restaurant."

Sarah's heart began to beat faster. She'd known that Justin's amnesia covered their relationship, but not that the two converged so precisely. His memory stopped just a few hours before their meeting. Could it be no more than coincidence?

"Do you recall anything about that reception?" she asked, trying to sound casual.

"Not a thing. I awoke in the hospital three months ago thinking it was tomorrow. I've heard about it. I've even seen a photograph that was taken that night, but it's like looking at a stranger.''

"What did the photograph show?"

"Jack Vernon and me standing together, wearing official smiles. He was trying to look as if he didn't hate my guts for stealing his firm.''

"Stealing?"

"That's how he saw it. I paid a good price, but he didn't really want to merge. I hadn't given him much choice.'' Justin stopped, looking into the middle distance at the things he'd discovered about himself that made him uncomfortable.

Something in his frown and far-off look made Sarah wonder if he was on the verge of remembering, and she was suddenly afraid. It was too soon. He was still too close to the old Justin. If he remembered now, he might leave her. Just a little longer, her heart pleaded. Just a little longer.

Chapter Four

The spell was broken by Nicky, who was beginning to take his first steps and wanted to test his skills. As he'd done before, he seized Justin's arm and hauled himself to his feet. Justin immediately gave him his attention, as if glad of an excuse to escape his thoughts.

"Go to Mommy," Justin urged. When Nicky had toddled the two steps to Sarah's open arms Justin moved to widen the distance between them. "To me," he said, laughing, and Nicky waddled on his stumpy legs, crowing with achievement.

"Come here, darling," Sarah called. Her eyes met Justin's in a moment of shared understanding. This was how she'd longed for things to be, how she'd thought they never would be.

Suddenly Nicky lost his balance and sat down with

a thump. The next moment he let out a deafening bawl. Sarah hurriedly picked him up. "Poor darling," she soothed. "Did you hurt yourself?"

But instead of letting her comfort him Nicky fought to be free, roaring louder than ever.

"Give him to me," Justin said, moving closer and lifting Nicky from her arms. "Hey, c'mon, now. There's nothing to cry about. You'll get the hang of it. Try it this way." He held Nicky upright so that his feet were on the ground but he was steadied by Justin's hands. Nicky's sobs quietened as he stamped his feet up and down and the look of concentration returned to his face. He seemed to understand that he was safe while Justin held him.

"It's not like him to cry like that," Sarah said worriedly. "I hope he isn't hurt."

"He's not hurt," Justin said with a grin. "Just good and mad. He was doing so well, and he's cross with himself for not doing better."

"And how do you know that, Mr. Baby Psychologist?"

"I was just the same. My mom used to tell me that, when I was learning to walk, I'd get so frustrated when I fell over I'd yell the place down. I wanted to be able to do it all at once. He's that way, too."

"Yes," Sarah said, half to herself. "He is."

"Well, I guess all babies are like that, aren't they?"

No, she thought. *Not all of them. But your son is like you.*

Nicky was making eager little grunts, stamping his feet. Justin released him, and he floundered to his mother, then back, and back again. But at last even he grew tired. Sarah took him in her arms and settled him against her.

"He's a great little kid," Justin said. "A fighter already, and he's going to grow up ready to take what he wants from the world." He saw a shadow cross her face. "What is it?"

"I'm just not sure that's what I wish for him. Surely there's more to life than taking from the world?"

"Of course. But you have to know how to take, or you'll be taken from. Fighting is good, Sarah. It's fight or be crushed." When she still looked troubled he said, "Don't you want Nicky to grow into a man folks respect?"

"Yes, but not because he can make them afraid of him. I want people to respect him because he's kind and good and gentle, and because he understands that people matter."

"Well, of course people matter but, well..."

"But you don't get on in the world by worrying about their feelings?" Sarah asked gently.

Justin reddened. She'd extended his words further than he liked, and done it so accurately it was as though she'd looked into his mind. Uneasily, he sensed that she wouldn't approve of everything she found there.

Hot, argumentative words rose to his lips. He'd always been impatient with those who disagreed with him, and he couldn't relax until he'd overcome them with argument. But something in Sarah's soft brown eyes made him fall silent. It was as though she'd withdrawn from him: only by a little, but he minded.

"I guess maybe I don't know what I'm talking

about,'' he said awkwardly. He was unpracticed in saying such things.

Sarah pulled on a blade of grass, not looking at him. ''I think when it comes to making people do what you want, you know exactly what you're talking about.''

''Hey, where did that come from?'' he demanded.

''Nowhere,'' she said quickly. ''I'm sorry. I had no right to say it. I daresay I'm wrong.''

''No,'' he said after a moment. ''You're not wrong. It's just kind of unnerving that you can understand me so well. I *am* like that. In business it's not a bad way to be—some of the time.''

Sarah felt she'd come close to revealing her secret knowledge. She cast around for a new and less dangerous subject. ''So anyway, your mom taught you to be an expert with babies?'' she said in a lighter, teasing tone.

He jumped as though the thought alarmed him. ''Expert? No way. I've got a younger brother, and there's seven years between us but I never had to look after him when he was a baby.''

But in a way he *had* looked after Greg, he realized. He'd taken him into his firm, swearing that his brother would never have to struggle as he had. He'd been protective, teaching him the things a businessman had to know, like efficiency, high standards and ruthlessness. Now he wondered if that was enough.

There were so many other things that mattered, like how it felt to lie back on a summer's day, smell the new-mown grass and drink coffee with a woman who was special. He'd never taught Greg that these were important, because until now he hadn't known. For the first time he wondered if his influence on his brother had been good.

The babble of the water and the warmth of the sun were hypnotic. He watched Sarah, her head bent over Nicky, who was grunting contentedly in her arms. As before, the sight of her sent cares from his mind, and the strain seemed to fall away from him.

"Listen to how he snores," she said softly. "He always makes that noise. I lie awake at night, listening. While I can hear him, I know everything's all right with the world."

He nodded. "It must be wonderful to have something like that, that can tell you the world's okay," he said a tad wistfully.

"Yes, it is. I think I'll put him down for his nap."

Justin pushed the portable crib toward her, drew back the blankets while she laid the sleeping tot inside, then pulled them into position over him. Sarah had adjusted the sunshade until she was sure Nicky was completely protected. Only when her mother's heart was satisfied did she look up to find that Justin had been watching her. And something in his eyes made her breath stop.

She thought he whispered her name, but she wasn't sure. Then she felt his fingertips touch her cheek gently. When he drew her toward him her heart sang with joy.

She could remember their last kiss vividly. It was the night he'd said, "I'll be busy for a while." And she had said goodbye, knowing that was what he really meant. He'd kissed her with a kind of angry impatience, as though he'd made a decision that troubled him but that needed to be made, and now he wanted to get it over with.

This time his lips on hers were tender, and his arms about her were warm, two qualities she'd seldom associated with Justin. Their love had been passionate, intense, but he'd never made time for the lingering moments that would have meant so much to her. His mouth moved slowly, caressingly, over hers.

"I've wanted to kiss you since the first day," he murmured. "Did you know?"

"I...I'm not sure. I haven't been sure of anything."

"I know what you mean." He tightened his arms, and there was no more talk as they clung together.

Sarah tried to be restrained, remembering that he thought this was their first kiss. But as the old, familiar desire flooded over her, restraint was swept away. For so long she'd ached for the feel of his body and the heat of his ardor. Now it was hers again, and she reveled in it. Whatever else might be different about him, the tangy, nutty smell that she loved was still the same. It brought back nights of passion and heart-stopping joy.

She didn't know how long her happiness would last, so she would seize it now, grateful for what she'd been given when all hope was gone. All her love was in her kiss. He sensed her eager response and held her closer, sliding his fingers through her soft hair.

Justin was caught up in bewilderment. Despite a desperate desire to kiss Sarah, he'd told himself not to. He didn't belong in this sleepy place with its limited horizons, and however much Sarah delighted him he knew he must leave her soon. He'd sorted all this out in his reasonable mind.

But his body's longing could brush his common sense aside so that nothing mattered but taking her in his arms and discovering the responsiveness of her mouth. And as soon as he held her he knew it was a mistake, for the bittersweet enchantment that possessed him was irresistible. Just one kiss, he'd told himself, and then he would break away. But he knew he couldn't break away until he'd enjoyed one more kiss, and then one more. And it would never end.

"Sarah," he murmured, "Sarah." Her name alone seemed to evoke the whole of life. The warmth and gentleness of the world seemed to be here, offering itself to him. All sweetness, all womanly tenderness was in his arms, *his*. He could drown himself in such beauty, lose himself forever and be glad of it.

But the thought was like a warning bell clamoring in his brain. He who'd always controlled people and events as a matter of self-preservation was letting that control slip away without even a fight.

He drew back to look at her face. It was beautiful, hazy with self-forgetting passion. She was as natural and spontaneous as earth, as fresh as spring water, as good and honest as the elements. She was dangerous.

Slowly he released her, fighting his heart's urge to draw her closer and say words that would commit him to her forever. "I guess this isn't the time or place," he said unsteadily.

"No," she whispered. "We should be getting home."

She said little on the journey, but sometimes she

turned to him with a look he couldn't bear to see, it was so full of confident happiness. The thought of what he was planning to do shamed him. It was a betrayal of her and what they'd shared for those few magic moments. It would have been easy to yield to that magic. Instead he was going to kill it.

They reached home to find Nick already philosophical about his Hepplewhite cabinet. Colly had called during the day and destroyed his fantasies with a few well-chosen words.

"Never mind, it's still beautiful," Sarah consoled him. There was a radiance about her that made everything she said seem significant.

After supper Justin said casually, "How far is it to Barton-on-sea?"

"About ten miles," Nick replied. "It's a popular place for trippers because the sand is lovely."

"I'll make that my next destination. Ten miles isn't too far for one day." He smiled at Sarah. "I've imposed on you long enough."

Her color faded, but all she said was, "It's no trouble. We like having you—"

"But I'm a lot of extra work, with the shop and all. I'll pay you up to the end of the week, but I'll leave tomorrow."

He was relieved to have the decision taken. His life lay elsewhere, among big things, important things and people, manipulating large amounts of money. He was shocked at himself for having come so close to falling in love with Sarah.

After the first protest she seemed to accept his decision, and next morning she made him sandwiches for the journey. "It's been nice having you here," she said politely. "Drop us a line sometime to let us know how you're going on."

"Of course I will," he said.

"Say goodbye, Nicky." She held the baby up, and Justin gently brushed the soft little cheek. Evidently considering this a new game, Nicky seized his fingers with astonishing strength.

"He's got a grip of iron, this one," Justin said, laughing.

"He likes you," Sarah said. "He doesn't want you to go." She added softly, "Nor do I."

"I've had a great time, but I should be moving on. Hey, Nicky, you don't give up, do you?"

With difficulty he disentangled himself. Sarah, hiding a breaking heart under a calm manner, wanted to shout, "Look at his hands. Can't you see how like your own they are?" But she stayed silent, because nothing would avail her now. A dramatic avowal of love, a last-minute disclosure of the truth—it was too late for either of them.

"Bye, little feller." He touched Nicky's cheek again, but the child understood what was happening and began to cry. "It's not that bad," Justin protested. "Let's say goodbye." He took Nicky into his arms, and the baby hushed at once. "We had some good times together, didn't we? I'll come back and see how you're doing. With that strength of yours, you'll probably be able to beat me arm wrestling."

You'll never come back, Sarah thought in despair. *Never.*

Justin returned Nicky to her. He immediately began to cry again, but differently this time, small, resigned sobs that shaded into sad hiccups. He was his mother's child and knew when a harsh truth had to be faced.

"Well, goodbye, sir." Justin shook Uncle Nick's hand. "Goodbye, Sarah. Thanks for everything."

He gave her a friendly nod and walked quickly away. Sarah watched him go, thinking of another goodbye. Only this one was far more final. She let her features relax, not caring what they showed now, but at the corner he turned and waved, and she quickly hid her face against Nicky.

Justin's way led over the hill that rose behind Haven. It was a hot, sunny day, and by the time he reached the top he was thirsty. He sat down to take out the bottle of mineral water he'd brought. The village lay spread out before him, details showing vividly in the clear air. He could see the vicarage, the garden filled with vegetables, carefully fenced to protect them from the sheep that grazed in the churchyard.

He told himself he'd been lucky to see the danger in time. Better to make the break now, before it was too late. But where a sense of relief should have been, there was only a crushing sensation that almost amounted to pain. It was like the baby's grip, which had been strong enough to hurt him. He'd freed himself from Nicky's hands, but not from the sound of his weeping.

He wished the ache in his heart would stop. It gave him a sense of apprehension, as though by denying it he was committing a monstrous crime. As though, once before...

He was beginning to dread those moments when memories flickered past, brushing his mind with tantalizing wings before vanishing. The fruitless efforts to capture them left him drained and close to despair. It was like that now. He tried saying to himself, "Once before, once before," but it was no good. His mind refused to give him what he sought.

He mustn't return to Sarah. Despite the passion that had flared up between them he'd sensed that she was still haunted by that other man. He'd never played second fiddle in his life, and he wasn't going to start now.

Then her face came into his mind, possessed by anguish, as it had been in the last moment, before she buried her face against her son.

There was only one answer to that kind of weakness, to put as much distance between them as possible. He walked until late afternoon, then found a small restaurant where he could eat under the trees.

He bought a national newspaper and tried to read it. But the stories of the big world to which he was returning, *his* world, seemed to dance before his eyes. Overhead he could hear a bird calling continuously. It was a sad sound, like the crying of a child or the stifled grief of a woman.

He finished his meal, left the restaurant and began to walk.

Losing Justin the second time was worse. Now Sarah knew it was really over. Perhaps, after all, the miracle wasn't meant to be.

She was dazed with the speed of it all. Only a few days, when she'd counted on so much more! When he said, "This isn't the time or place," she'd thought she understood him. He would come to her that night and they would rediscover each other in the sweetness of passion. And perhaps, lying in her arms, he would remember and truly return to her. That had been the dream that made her radiant. His casual decision to depart had been like a blow in the face. She'd lain awake all that night, listening for him, hoping in the face of despair, knowing that he wouldn't come. Her body had ached for him, but not as much as her heart. Now she saw herself clearly, a self-deluding fool who'd read something into a chance encounter because she wanted to.

Uncle Nick showed his sympathy by sending her away from the shop, giving her time to concentrate on little Nicky. There was some comfort in hugging this little piece of Justin to her heart.

She went to bed early and slept lying on her stomach, her arm drooping over the side of the bed, so that her fingers touched Nicky's cheek. She stayed like that until two in the morning, when she was awoken by the doorbell. She got up, rubbing her eyes, knowing that Uncle Nick, who was a heavy sleeper, would never awake. She made her way drowsily downstairs and opened the door.

For a long moment she and Justin looked at each other in silence. His face told the story of his struggle and his bewildered, uncomprehending return. There was a question in his eyes, which Sarah answered by opening her arms.

"I'm sorry to drag you out of bed," he murmured, crushing her against him. "I'd gone a long way when I knew I had to come back. Sarah, I—"

"Hush," she said.

"But I must tell you— Hell, I don't know how to say it, or even what to say."

"Don't try. Don't try."

They held each other tightly, then she took his hand and drew him upstairs, where sounds were coming from Nicky's cot. Justin knelt so that the child could see his face. "Hallo, little feller," he said softly. "Think I wasn't coming back?"

Light broke over Nicky's face, and he reached out chubby arms. As Justin held him close Sarah gave thanks from a full heart. She watched with delight as her child fell asleep again in his father's arms, as though that was all he needed to be content.

"I guess I just couldn't go away and leave him crying like that," Justin said, laying Nicky in his cot and tucking him in.

"I'm glad you couldn't." She followed him out of the room and closed the door quietly. "I'll make your bed up again."

While she did so he unpacked his things. Suddenly he blurted, "Hell, no, I'm a liar. I didn't just come back for Nicky. I came for you. I couldn't leave you, Sarah."

She was in his arms in a moment, kissing him eagerly. He responded with a kind of passionate relief, as though admitting the truth had freed him.

"Are you glad I'm back, Sarah?"

"Yes. Yes. Why did you go?"

"I don't know," he said fiercely. "I must have been crazy."

She pressed her body against his, longing for the perfect physical union she'd known with him before. And this time it would be so much better, now that he had a heart to give, as well. She'd meant to be cautious, but she couldn't manage it. She wanted him heart, body and soul, and she was ready to claim him again,

Justin could feel her slim, rounded shape beneath the thin cotton of her nightdress, inciting him to madness. A moment ago he'd been exhausted after his long walk, but the thought of making love with her made new life stream through him.

"Sarah, Sarah..."

She couldn't answer in words, but her trembling breath told him all he needed to know. He lifted her and laid her gently on the bed, kissing her again and again. Her body seemed to become pure flame on the instant, all flickering excitement and eagerness. She began to pull his shirt out of his belt, and he helped her, tossing his clothes aside feverishly. Illness had left him thinner, but his body was still the one she remembered and passionately loved. She ran her hands over his shoulders, his arms, his chest, thrilling as she sensed that the power was still there.

"Now you," he whispered in a voice heavy with desire. "I want to see you."

He drew her nightdress over her head, and Sarah threw her head back, reveling in her body's freedom.

She felt herself drawn close as he rained fierce kisses on her heated skin, and she gave herself up to him, gloriously shameless in her passion. Her body had been created for this one man, and she made a joyful gift of herself.

Her flesh had slept, but now it was alive to his lightest caress, eager for the pleasure only he could bring. A soft moan of desire broke from her as she felt the urgency in her loins. She wanted him so much.

Justin caressed her slowly, savoring the pleasure of discovering her. She was all he'd imagined, soft and ripe, with the generous curves of a woman of the earth. She smelled of all the good things in nature, dark, rich, welcoming.

He'd thought he knew Sarah, but he hardly knew her at all. He loved the little touch of shyness that she brought to everyday life, but he found to his delight that she wasn't shy as a lover. With the man who'd won her confidence she was blazingly eager, instantly responsive. The touch of his lips on one proud nipple sent a shudder of ecstasy through her slim body. She arched against him, murmuring his name in a way that inflamed him. The swelling softness of her breasts ravished his senses. He wanted to bury his face against their silky skin, caressing them with his eager mouth.

Sarah felt the insistent provocation of his lips and tongue as ripples of pleasure pervaded her from top to toe. She loved the feel of his hands seeking her, touching her with a skill and subtlety that was deliciously seductive.

"How could I go away from you?" he whispered. "How could I do it? Was I mad?"

She tried to reply, but the blood was pulsing so madly in her veins she could only give a soft little moan. Her eyes answered him, glowing with the fever of passion only he could create, and her fingers answered, gliding down the length of his hard body and rediscovering the shape she loved. Despite the long parting, this was still the man whose clever hands and powerful loins had brought her ecstasy. He was using his fingers to trace soft patterns on her inner thigh, inciting in her a fever of anticipation.

The old instincts were still there, telling her of the urgency of his need, but also telling her he was holding back until he was sure of her. She could feel the hardness of his manhood as he moved slowly over her, settling between her legs, taking it easy, letting her set the pace. Only when he sensed her impatience did he drive forward, entering her slowly but purposefully. The pleasure was great, but more than pleasure was a sense that all was well. He'd tried to leave, but the force that linked him to her was stronger than he was, and now they both knew he was where he belonged.

Sarah found the feel of Justin inside her unbearably good. She clung to him, moving her hips with his powerful thrusts. They'd always been in tune, finding each other's rhythm easily, and it was still true. Heat spread through her body. She felt like pure flame, flickering and dancing in a furnace of desire.

For Justin the sensation of their rightness together was wonderful. His body seemed to know the caresses that would bring her the most pleasure. The intensity of her desire for him made him feel like a god. The sight of her lying there, her hair splayed on the pillow, her eyes hazy as they looked into his, seared him with tenderness. Her vulnerability terrified him. Yet there was also power in the way she came back at him, giving passion for passion, driving him on to love her more deeply.

"Justin...Justin...oh, yes..."

"Yes, sweetheart," he murmured. "Tell me that you want me."

"Always." The word was little more than a sigh, but his heart heard it. He laid his face against her neck and felt her arms enfold him.

Somewhere deep inside her the pleasure was gathering momentum, spinning her around so fast that she lost her bearings. All she knew was that she was part of a whirling universe. She and he were one, and that was how it had been meant to be since the dawn of time.

She cried out when her moment came because she knew what she would lose when she seemed to gain everything. There was a price to be paid for such sweet fulfillment, and last time she'd paid it in tears and loneliness. But there was no way back, nothing but to give herself utterly to the explosive ecstasy they found together. It wasn't her nature to offer only half of herself. As they reached the heights, she felt herself melting into him and was rewarded by the totality of his returning gift.

As she returned to reality Sarah waited for Justin to leave her, as he'd always done before, impatient to resume his business, even after love.

But he didn't move. His head was heavy between her breasts. She enfolded it tenderly, stroking his hair, awed by the beauty of what she'd found again. At last she realized he had gone to sleep, holding her like a man who'd come safely to a place of refuge.

Justin discovered he was in a strange place. All around him was a mist, and something seemed to drag at his feet, holding him back. On one side was a brick wall that he touched as he felt his way forward. Suddenly the wall turned a corner. His heart leaped as he understood what he sought was just around that corner. Only a little farther to go now.

But at the last moment he found his way blocked by a man with his own face.

Chapter Five

Nick greeted Justin's reappearance without surprise. Perhaps he didn't sleep as heavily as Sarah thought. All he said next morning was, "Nice to see you back. I need someone to drive to the wholesalers. Sarah, you go, too, and show him the way. Any tea going?"

They collected the goods and stopped in a farmhouse tea shop on the way back. The tables were under the trees, and they drank their tea accompanied by clucking chickens who'd learned where the pickings were good.

"I had the strangest dream last night," Justin said with a touch of awkwardness.

"What happened?" Sarah asked, wondering if their reunion had restored some of his memory.

"I dreamed that I tried to leave you, but I couldn't. My feet turned themselves around in the road and made me walk back. And you were there, waiting for me, and you were all I thought you'd be.'' He met her eyes, a touch of diffidence in his own. "It wasn't a dream, was it, Sarah?''

"If it was, I was dreaming the same dream.''

"I was afraid it was just my own wishful thinking.''

"And mine,'' she said, smiling.

In a short time Justin felt like a fixture in Haven. It wasn't just his growing passion for Sarah. It was that her presence gave him a feeling of safety, as though she knew a secret he must learn from her. He'd never wanted safety in the past, but sometimes these days he felt like a drowning man with only her to cling to. At other times he knew only the glad certainty that she was there, and therefore all was right with the world.

He began to help out with the shop. The first time he was left to cope on his own was a chastening experience. Being able to carry huge, complex deals in his head was little preparation for coping with people who wanted half a pound of cheese, the nice dark one—no, the other one over there—well, perhaps I won't bother.

There were a thousand small items, and a thousand different prices, and he survived only because his customers knew the stock better than he did, and were kind.

It was while serving behind the counter that he made Joker's acquaintance. Joker was sixteen and about to leave school. He was bright, bored and came marked Trouble with a capital *T*. Justin both liked and mistrusted him from the first moment.

Before long his sharp eyes caught Joker shoplifting. It was always small items worth a few pennies, and he correctly deduced that the boy was doing it for the thrill and to impress his gang. "Why do you bother?" he demanded, exasperated. "I always catch you."

"That's the fun," Joker said. "No point if it's too easy."

"Can't you get your kicks some other way than robbing shopkeepers who can't afford it?"

"I don't rob 'em." Joker was shocked. "I always give the stuff back—well, I do if I don't get caught taking it. Putting it back's as hard as pinching it. What else is there to do around here?"

Sarah was sympathetic when Justin told her. "He's right. Young people escape Haven as soon as they can. Like me, some of them come back later, when they've discovered how valuable this little place is. But one day I'm afraid there'll be nothing to come back to."

Justin's new skills included baby-sitting Nicky. Toddlers had never attracted him, but this one had claimed him as his own, and there was something about the child's delight in his company that Justin couldn't resist.

Under Sarah's cooking his body filled out again. To regain his strength he began hiring a horse from a nearby riding school. When she could Sarah joined him, and they explored the lovely countryside together. It was perfect weather for riding, warm and sunny, but not hot enough to be unpleasant. The land was at its best, glowing with all the colors of summer.

"We can take a shortcut to the woods by going across Merton's Farm," she said. "There's a right-of-way, although a lot of people don't use it because Will Merton always makes himself unpleasant.''

Merton was a weaselly little man with a whining voice and sharp eyes. He scowled but didn't try to stop them. Halfway across his farm they stopped to greet a very large, shabbily dressed man. Sarah introduced him as Hal Jones, one of Merton's farmhands. "Was the boss awkward about you coming through?" he asked cheerfully.

"As usual," Sarah said. "I don't know why he makes such a fuss. We all stick to the paths and take care not to hurt his crops."

"Such as they are," Justin observed, looking around him. "I'm no farmer, but surely the crop ought to look better than this?"

"He won't buy decent fertilizer," Hal confided. "I worked here a few years ago, for his dad. It was a good farm then, but I left when Will took over. I had to come back because jobs are scarce, and it breaks my heart. He squeezes every penny out of this place, but he's too mean to put any back in, so it's going to rack and ruin. The crop's such rubbish that even the birds aren't interested. Ol' Timmy Bags has nowt to do these days.''

"Timmy Bags?" Justin echoed.

Hal pointed to the center of a field where a woebegone scarecrow flapped about. "He's been there for years," he said. "I dunno how he came to be called Timmy Bags, but it's always been his name."

"'Ere, you—Hal!" They all turned to see Will Merton standing in the lane, waving furiously. "Do I pay you to stand about gabbing?" he yelled.

"You barely pays me at all," Hal muttered. "Mean ol' scroat. Coming, Mr. Merton." He gave Sarah and Justin a cheery wave and moved down the lane.

Half a mile farther on Justin stopped and said, "I don't believe what I'm seeing."

Through a gap in the trees they could discern a beautiful Tudor house. The walls were made of black timbers with white inserts. The red tiled roof glowed in the sun, and tall chimneys reached up to the sky.

"It's Merton's farmhouse," Sarah said. "I delivered something there once, and it's just as beautiful inside, except that he doesn't take proper care of it."

"It's a crime a jewel like that belongs to Will Merton."

"He hates it. He'd like to knock it down, but it's been officially registered as a building of historical interest, so he can't."

They left the farm behind and rode into the country. They found a stream to water the horses, and sat entwined in each other's arms. Passion would come later, but moments like these were equally precious. Sarah could sense the deep, physical content that pervaded Justin, and which came from simply being with her. His face was relaxed. She realized how often it was that way now, and wondered at the power that had forced him to turn on the road and come back to her. She felt caught up in something greater than her own understanding. But whatever it was, for now she was content to leave her fate in its hands.

When he discovered that Sarah spent three nights a week rehearsing with the Haven Players, Justin joined them, too. This led to his meeting another village institution, the Grainger sisters, Lila and Thetis. They were in their sixties, one divorced, one unmarried. They lived together and made ends meet by running a baby-sitting service. The scarcity of teenagers made them much in demand, and when there was a gathering parents would first make their way to the Grainger cottage, bearing infants. Without these two women the social life of Haven would have ground to a halt.

On Sarah's rehearsal nights Nick often looked after the baby. But sometimes Nicky would be delivered to the Graingers, who adored him, so that Nick could enjoy an evening in the Haystack, playing Colly at chess, calling him rude names and receiving ruder ones in return.

Justin's first night with the drama society was an ordeal he was never to forget. Mrs. Lucinda Cates, the leader, called for quiet and climbed onto the tiny stage to address them. She was a portly little woman with gray hair and an arch manner. "We're welcoming a new member tonight," she announced. "His name's Justin, and here he is."

There was applause as Justin stood up, trying not to look sheepish.

"Now, Justin, we need to know what you can do," Lucinda went on, "so I've got a scene here for you to read through."

He just stopped himself exclaiming, "Act?" in tones of dismay. After all, it was what he was supposed to be here to do.

"You don't mind doing a teensy weensy little audition, do you?" Lucinda asked waggishly. "All the greatest actors had to start that way, you know."

"Oh, er, yes, of course," he said hastily. "It's just that I saw myself in more of a backstage role—painting scenery, and—and carrying things." A flash of sublime idiocy made him add, "I'm very good at carrying things." He fell silent, feeling desperately that he was making a fool of himself. A titter from behind him confirmed it.

"Of course," Lucinda agreed. "But one of our members has dropped out of *Laughing All the Way,* and we need a replacement. You must imagine that you're Frank, talking to Amy. Sarah's playing Amy, so she'll read the scene with you. Take a moment to look it over."

Justin read the scene and was aghast to find it was a declaration of love. But it was too late to back out. He went hot with embarrassment. It was worse when he was standing with Sarah on the stage. He felt horribly exposed.

Sarah began, "I heard you wanted to see me, Frank."

"I never get a chance to talk to you, Amy," he managed to say. "So now I'm going to say it all at once." His voice sounded hollow. It was a relief to get to the end of the line.

"Say what, Frank?" Sarah recited. "You make it sound important."

He took a deep breath and plunged into the avowal of love. He knew he was dreadful. He was worse than dreadful, he was abysmal. His body was awkward, and he had no control over his voice. He stumbled through to the end, wishing the earth would open and swallow him up.

Fortunately Lucinda was a merciful woman. "Thank you, Justin," she said. "That was very, er, very... We have lots of scenery that needs painting."

There was a chuckle from the others, and for an instant Justin was furious. Nobody was allowed to laugh at him. He was on the verge of uttering an icy comment when he caught Sarah's eye. She was smiling sympathetically, and he suddenly knew he was at a crisis point. Sarah would expect a man to be able to take a joke against himself. Drawing on all his reserves of self-discipline, he forced himself to smile. "Don't forget carrying things," he said. "That's my specialty."

This time the laugh was warmer. He'd passed the first test. Good nature. These people valued it.

Red-faced, he took his seat beside Sarah. She squeezed his hand. "I think you're very brave," she said.

"Go away," he growled. "Let a man suffer in peace."

Sarah looked at him tenderly. She'd seen everything, including the moment when he nearly lost his temper. She remembered the speech he'd made at the reception the night they met. He'd been poised, self-confident, a far cry from the awkward amateur of this evening. His audience had laughed at his well-crafted witticisms, but no one would have dared to laugh at *him*.

He was still the man she'd seen that night, as his gleam of annoyance proved, but he'd mastered it. It was as though he had different priorities now.

"What about me, Lucinda?" Alex Drew stood up,

radiating assurance with his flashy good looks. "I'll play Frank."

"You're already playing the comic gardener," Lucinda objected.

"But they don't meet. It's only one scene, and I'll have time to change." He gave a charming grin. "And then the audience will say, 'What a brilliant actor that Alex Drew must be!'"

"All right," Lucinda said. "Let's give it a try."

Sarah returned to the stage and read the scene again. To Justin's chagrin Alex did it beautifully. He was a natural actor who made the trite lines sound good. Sarah was no more than competent, but with his skillful partnership she flowered. Justin ground his teeth.

"Very well, Alex, you've got the part," Lucinda called from the back of the hall.

"Hooray!" Alex did a little jig. "I've been wanting the chance to make love to Sarah." He seized her and bent her back against his arm in a theatrical simulation of a passionate kiss.

"Get off, you idiot!" she said, laughing.

"She spurns me! Calamity!" Alex struck his forehead and staggered away to throw himself against the wall as if distraught. The company cheered the bravura performance.

Justin stayed in the shadows, hoping his feelings didn't show on his face. It had been only in fun, of course. But if Alex had held Sarah a moment longer, he knew he couldn't have answered for his own actions.

Miss Timmins was the stage manager, and Justin was made her assistant. "I hope you don't mind such a lowly position," she said doubtfully. "You don't look to me as though you're used to taking orders."

"I am," he said quickly. "Where I work, I'm just the tea boy, I swear it."

"Hmm!" Her bright, intelligent eyes regarded him.

"Look, as long as nobody asks me to get up there and act…"

"Don't worry," she said kindly. "After that audition, nobody will." They laughed together.

"What does the assistant stage manager have to do?" he asked.

"All the jobs nobody else wants."

"That's what I thought," he said with a grin.

Justin soon developed a hearty respect for Miss Timmins. She had a clear head and a grasp of detail he could have used in his firm. She judged the world and everyone in it by the yardstick of the fitness of things. It was a phrase she never explained, but Justin gathered that it covered everything. If Miss Timmins judged someone to have no sense of the fitness of things, that someone was beyond redemption.

His dislike of Alex grew daily. Alex constantly had the company in fits with his antics, including, Justin was annoyed to notice, Sarah. The boy had been spoilt since the day he was born, and whatever he wanted he thought was his by right. He could have had his pick of any of Haven's young woman, several of whom had joined the Players to be near him. But it seemed to Justin's jealous eyes that he homed in on Sarah.

Someone else had noticed it, too. Imelda Drew, Alex's mother, occasionally dropped in to rehearsals, explaining that, as a member of the parish council, she had a responsibility to ensure that the hall was used only for proper purposes. This fooled nobody.

The tea break would arrive and Justin would hand around plastic cups as meekly as a waiter. Imelda would address Sarah with overpowering graciousness before urging Alex not to be home late, "because Lousia is dropping in." To the others she would explain that Lousia was "an heiress, but such a sweet unspoilt girl. Alex and she are so fond of each other." Her eyes, focused on Sarah, would be like gimlets.

"I don't know how you stand that woman," Justin said one night as they left the rehearsal.

Sarah shrugged. "I feel sorry for her. She's so obvious. And she's wasting her efforts. I haven't set my cap at her little boy."

"You were laughing at him hard enough tonight."

"Of course I was. Alex is very funny. But that's all."

"Are you sure that's all?" he growled.

Sarah squeezed his arm. It felt so sweet to know he was jealous. "Oh, stop making a mountain out of a molehill," she said.

Most of the company went to the Haystack, but Sarah headed straight home to release Uncle Nick from baby-sitting duties. "Has he been all right?" she asked as she went in.

"Fine. Not a peep all evening. Now if you don't mind, I'll be off for a pint. Coming, Justin?"

"Thanks, but I'm worn out after an evening under Miss Timmins's command."

Sarah went to look in on Nicky, who was sleeping

peacefully. When she returned Justin was cooking the supper. "Mmm, lovely!" she said, sniffing appreciatively.

He made baked beans and toast, almost the only thing he knew how to cook. As they washed up he said, "You're very quiet. What's wrong?"

"Sorry, my mind's still on the play. I just can't get the hang of that scene. Alex says we should practise it together. Maybe it'll come right then."

"You're going to practise with Alex?" he asked in a hollow voice.

"I've got to rehearse it with someone."

"Right. But not with Alex. Me."

"But you're a terrible actor," she blurted before she could stop herself. At once she clapped her hand over her mouth. "I'm sorry," she said guiltily. "I've got this shocking way of making tactless remarks. I try not to, but they seem to come out anyway."

"Don't try," he said with a grin. "It's true. But I'll just be your stooge so you can say the lines."

"Fine. Thank you." She handed him the book, took up her position, and recited, "I heard you wanted to see me, Frank."

"I never get a chance to talk to you, Amy," he read. "So now I'm going to say it all at once." It was easier without an audience.

"Say what, Frank?" Sarah responded. "You make it sound important."

"Wait a minute," Justin stopped her. "I should stand closer, then we're not shouting to each other from opposite sides of the room."

"But Lucinda says Amy and Frank should stand apart," she objected.

"I'm just trying to create a natural atmosphere."

They tried again.

"This is useless," Justin said after a while. "He should simply cut the cackle and take her in his arms. If he had, she wouldn't have gone off with the other fellow in the end."

"Frank isn't a decisive character. He just couldn't do such a thing."

"But I could," Justin said firmly, tossing the book aside and taking her into his arms.

"You planned this all the time, didn't you?" she asked, laughing.

"Sure did. I'm a devious character." He began to kiss her neck, just beneath her ear, making shivers of pleasure go through her. "You don't really like that young puppy, do you?" he murmured. "You were just teasing me?"

"I wasn't teasing you," she said, speaking with difficulty through the hammering of her heart. "Oh, Justin, you fool. I never think of Alex...only of you."

"Good," he said against her mouth. "Let's keep it that way."

"*Halloo!*"

They jumped apart at the sound of Nick's voice below. "It's only me," he called. "I'll lock up."

"I like Nick a lot," Justin said in a shaking voice. "But he has no sense of timing."

"Colly must have beaten him at chess," Sarah said distractedly.

"Then curse Colly and all his works." He straightened his hair, feeling like a guilty teenager.

Nick came in. If he noticed anything in the air he gave no sign of it, but chatted away about his evening. Justin, still physically on edge, could have done without it, but he was fond of the old man, and he settled down with a look of intense interest. Sarah slipped away to check Nicky, who was just awaking.

"He couldn't have done that once," she confided to the baby. "I can remember when, if it didn't make him some money, he didn't want to know."

"What's that?" Justin was in the doorway.

"I was telling him a bedtime story," Sarah said hastily. "Has Nick gone to bed yet?"

"No, he wants a game of chess. Apparently *he* beat Colly, and he wants to tell me just how he did it."

"Oh, darling, I'm sorry."

"Don't be. There's a notice on the wall of my—the place I used to work. It says, It's never too late to learn a new skill. Seems like my day for learning patience." He kissed her nose good-humoredly. "Good night, Sarah. Don't wait up. I couldn't tell you how long I'm going to be, but if I'm not in bed by four in the morning, send out a search party."

One morning when Nick had just driven off to the wholesaler, Sarah said, "I've got to see Brenda about our new advertisement for the local news sheet. Can you manage on your own for a while?"

"Yes, ma'am. I may not be bright, but I'm willing."

She gave him a swift, tender kiss. "Councillor Norton will probably drop in for his order this morning. It's all packed up, over there. And if Denton's calls I'll have twice as much as usual. Right, Nicky, my love. Let's be off.''

But the baby reached out his fat arms to Justin. ''Leave him with me,'' he suggested. ''I'm great at looking after him now.''

''Well, it would certainly be easier.''

''Come on, Nicky,'' Justin said, taking him from her. ''You and I can enjoy some man talk.''

But almost as soon as they were alone, the delivery from Denton's arrived. ''Sarah's not here,'' Justin told the pleasant middle-aged man who came into the shop, ''but she wants twice her usual order—whatever it is.''

''Ice cream,'' the man said cheerfully. ''The best for miles. I'm Terry, by the way. Twice as much of everything, coming up.''

When Justin had helped him carry the cartons inside and store them in the deep freeze Terry produced a small tub of ice cream. ''Nicky's favorite,'' he said. ''Banana. Have some yourself.'' He offered two small wooden scoops.

Justin tried it, and his expression changed to one of astonishment at the most delicious taste he'd ever known. This was the real thing. ''That's fantastic,'' he said. ''Did Sarah order some of this? If not, I'll order some for myself.''

''Don't worry, she ordered plenty.'' Terry added somewhat wryly, ''Sarah's not the only one who gave me a double order. It's odd how knowing we may be closing down concentrates everyone's mind.''

"Closing down? Are you crazy? Don't tell me people don't buy this stuff."

"Oh, yes. We've got all the work we can handle, and then more. In fact there's a backlog, people are getting impatient."

"So take on more staff."

"More staff means more and better equipment. My machines are on their last legs. I need investment and bigger premises, but I can't produce conclusive figures to show that it would be economic, so the bank won't help. I can't afford to expand, but if I don't I'll go under."

Justin nodded. He was familiar with the pattern.

"Anyway, I can't stay here talking. Nice to meet you." Terry departed, leaving Justin thoughtful.

Nicky was excellent company. When there was a lull in the customers they passed the time with a walking lesson, then consumed more ice cream. Nicky contrived to get most of his around his mouth, which struck him as very funny. Justin wiped him clean, and found that Nicky was eyeing him with a twinkle. "You're a mess," he said severely, and got a contented gurgle in reply.

As he lifted the child Nicky steadied himself by putting his arms about Justin's neck. And then the strangest thing happened. A feeling unlike any he'd known before swept over Justin. It was both physical and emotional, a tenderness so powerful it had a primeval, animal quality. There were two strands intermingled, the gentle and the violent, gentleness for the child and a readiness to kill anyone who harmed him.

Now he understood the look he'd seen on Sarah's

face when she'd held her baby. He held the little body tighter and rested his cheek against the silky hair.

The phone rang. Justin answered with one hand and heard a man's voice. "Councillor Norton here. My order should have been delivered by now."

"I thought you were calling for it."

"Oh, no, no, no, no, *no!*" the man said rapidly. "I don't have time for that. Busy man, you know. Busy man. It's one of the penalties of public service. One's time isn't one's own. One makes the sacrifice gladly but one does expect a little help from those for whom the sacrifice is made."

"Er—does one?" Justin was treading carefully, anxious not to offend one of Sarah's customers. Evidently he'd made the wrong reply, because a testy note entered Councillor Norton's voice.

"Young man, are you trying to be funny?"

"Not at all," Justin said hastily, turning to stop Nicky plundering the counter. "I'm alone now, but I'll deliver your goods as soon as Sarah returns. Can I have your address?"

"Everyone knows where I live," Councillor Norton snapped, and hung up. Justin breathed out and counted to ten.

"You know that guy?" he demanded of Nicky. The child made a sound that might have been a raspberry. "Yes, that's how I feel."

Nicky solemnly offered Justin a present. He accepted it and found himself holding a handful of ice cream.

"Thank you," he said, since his appreciation was

clearly expected. "What am I supposed to do with that?"

Nicky grinned. *That's your problem.*

Justin stared. For an astounding moment he'd almost thought the child had spoken to him. Of course, that was impossible, but Nicky's expression made his thoughts clear.

Justin firmly pressed the gift back into the tiny hand. "Now it's your problem," he said. "Get out of that."

For answer Nicky hurled the ice cream across the shop. It landed on the clock face, where Justin would have to clean it. Nicky met his eyes. *My point, I think.*

"Oh, yeah? You think that's funny?"

A gurgle. *I think it's very funny.*

"Just wait. I'll get even."

A dismissive grunt. *In your dreams.*

"You're not the only one who can throw ice cream, you know."

But I'm the only one who can hit the clock.

"You think! You see this fresh tub? I'm going to take the top off—like this—squash the ice cream in my hand until it's the rough consistency of yuk! Then I'm going to throw it and hit the—oops!"

"What's going on?" Sarah asked, wiping her eye.

"We were having a contest," Justin explained with as much dignity as he could muster in the circumstances. "It's called, 'Let's splatter Mommy with ice cream.'"

Nicky snorted. *Liar.*

"All right, all right. Actually I was aiming for the clock."

"Justin, I'm probably going to regret asking this, but why were you throwing ice cream at the clock?"

"Trying to get a bull's-eye, of course."

"Of course. I should have thought of that."

"Nicky managed it. You don't think I'm going to be defeated by a toddler, do you?"

Sarah's lips twitched. "He's had more practise than you. He throws things at the clock all the time. I only asked you to mind the shop. I didn't say anything about ice-cream-throwing contests."

"He started it," Justin said defensively. He gave a grin that made her heart turn over, and the next moment they were laughing together.

"I'll swear that kid talked to me," he said. "Not in words but—I don't know. It was like I could read his mind." He saw her smiling. "I guess that happens to you all the time, but you're his mother. How come I can read him so easily?"

"Because he wanted you to," Sarah said, sliding away from the dangerous subject. "Nicky has his own ways of getting his meaning across."

"That must be it." He wasn't sure whether to tell her about the powerful sensation of bittersweet tenderness that had swept him, but he backed off because he couldn't have put it into words.

Sarah sighed when he described Councillor Norton's call. "Oh, dear! He's up to his tricks again. I made it very clear he'd have to collect his own stuff. He's only two streets away, in Hanmere Lane."

"But he's too much of a big shot to come in person. He told me so. I got a lecture on the sacrifices of public service."

"Poor little man," Sarah said ruefully. "He's the leader of the parish council."

"How big is the council?"

"Only five. There's Mr. Norton, and Imelda Drew, and three others nobody ever sees. They're businessmen who live around here but work miles away. They just rubber-stamp whatever the other two tell them. It's the most important thing that's ever happened to Mr. Norton, and I'm afraid it's gone to his head."

"I'll do the delivery. I'm curious to meet him."

Hanmere Lane was at the prosperous end of Haven. Everard Norton lived in a well-kept, picture-book cottage with a thatched roof and hollyhocks growing around the door. In the front a large notice proudly proclaimed Councillor Norton's Residence. Justin knocked, and a man appeared at a window. He was plump, with an almost bald head and steel spectacles, and he looked cross.

"This is not the tradesmen's entrance," he said. "Kindly go to the rear." He closed the window.

Justin went around the tiny house and found the same man waiting for him at the back door. "I can't have deliveries made at the front," he said in a petulant voice, ushering Justin into the kitchen. "It disturbs people who come to see me for advice."

"I hope I haven't bothered whoever's there now."

Councillor Norton reddened slightly. "As a matter of fact there's nobody here now, but there might have been. I'm a public figure, on call night and day. I need some consideration. Let's have a look." He inspected the box, removing tea, sugar, a box of cigars. "I hope everything's here."

"Sarah assures me that it is."

Norton sniffed. "It all seems to be in order." He sounded disappointed. "Well, what are you waiting for?"

"The money," Justin explained. "This bit of paper is the bill."

Norton adjusted his spectacles. "Of course it's the bill," he snapped. "I can see it's the bill." He made no move to pay it.

"I thought perhaps you hadn't noticed it," Justin said. He'd rapidly taken in the details of the expensive kitchen. Councillor Norton could afford to pay his bills.

Norton breathed hard. "I shall settle my account the next time I come to the shop."

"But you're too busy for that," Justin reminded him. "An important public figure like you can't waste time—"

"Young man, are you being deliberately impertinent, or are you just plain stupid?"

"I'm not sure," Justin said gravely.

"Be very careful. Jobs are hard to come by these days, as you'll discover if I'm forced to complain to Miss Conroy about your manners."

Justin couldn't resist. "I hope you won't do that, sir," he said humbly.

"Hmm, that's as may be. Be off with you."

Justin departed while he could still keep a straight face, but his laughter faded as he neared the store, and by the time he arrived he was in a temper.

"You shouldn't let him get away with it," he stormed.

"Well, he pays in the end. He just likes to make me wait for it, and he always tries to beat the bill down."

"I don't know how you can call him a poor little man. He's a pompous idiot and as vain as hell. And for all his talk about serving the community, he's out of touch. He thought I worked for you, which makes him the only person in Haven who hadn't heard I was your lodger. The others knew everything about me, down to my sock size, long before we'd met."

Two evenings later, as he was about to close the shop for the night, he saw a gleaming, chauffeur-driven Rolls-Royce gliding to a halt outside. In the back seat was a man in his forties with a thin moustache and a weaselly face. With him was Councillor Everard Norton.

"Hey, Sarah, get this," Justin called.

She joined him at the door. "The Rolls belongs to Cyril Coverdale," she said. "He trains racehorses about three miles away. He often escorts Mr. Norton to council meetings."

"Is he a councillor, too?"

"No, I think he just does it to be nice."

Councillor Norton descended on the little shop. "You'll forgive me, my dear Sarah," he said loftily, "if I delay you from closing for a moment. I'm on my way to a *most* important council meeting, but I just had to stop and pay my bill, since I've been practically accused of trying to evade my financial obligations." His eyes rested on Justin.

"I'm sure nobody suggested such a thing," Sarah said soothingly.

"Would that they had not!" Norton exclaimed sorrowfully. "If only I could believe that I'd imagined the whole thing, the sly hints, the suggestion that I might flee the country—"

Justin choked but held his tongue. Norton sailed on.

"I accept such slings and arrows as part of being in public life. I bear no grudges. Here is the money I owe you."

Sarah took the money and flicked through it, frowning slightly. "I'm afraid it's not quite enough," she said.

"Your bill was incorrect, my dear Sarah. The cigars you charged me for were not there."

"Yes, they were," Justin said immediately. "I remember you taking them out when you inspected the delivery." He smiled blandly. "You must have forgotten."

Councillor Norton pressed his lips tightly together before replying. "If you say so," he conceded at last. "I'm a man of many cares. My mind is constantly occupied with the welfare of Haven. It's easy to make these small errors." Reluctantly he dug into his pocket and produced the missing money, refusing to meet Justin's eye.

Sarah poured oil on troubled waters. "I expect you've been hard at work for tonight's meeting. You're going to license the hall for *Laughing All the Way,* aren't you?"

For a moment the councillor was caught off guard. "Are we? Is that tonight? I thought the next meeting—"

"The next meeting is after the performance," Sarah reminded him. "It's tonight or never."

"Then I'm sure we can find the time for it," Norton declared grandly. "In the press of major affairs, let us never forget the small details."

"It wouldn't be a small detail if the Haven Players saw their hard work go for nothing just because you forgot their license," Justin pointed out.

Norton treated him to a frosty gaze. "I don't recall anyone asking you to speak, young man."

"I don't wait to be asked."

"Perhaps, Sarah, you should be a little more careful who you employ."

"I don't employ Justin," Sarah said. "He's our lodger, and he helps out in the shop. Isn't that kind of him?"

The discovery that he wasn't dealing with a menial didn't please Norton, but he was too wise to pursue an argument he couldn't win. Justin was no longer looking at him. He was watching Cyril Coverdale, who'd gotten out of the Rolls and was staring at the shop impatiently. After a moment he came in.

"Don't be offended if the license seemed to slip my mind," Norton was saying. "There are things being discussed tonight which—well, I mustn't betray confidences. But this I will say. Haven's day has come."

"Are you ready, Everard?" Coverdale asked him. He gave the other two a smile that seemed meant to be genial, but was merely chilly. Norton became a little flustered.

"Oh, er, yes, of course." He slipped out of the shop

and was swallowed up by the Rolls, which glided away.

"If Coverdale's just being nice, I'm a Dutchman," Justin observed. "I've met his type too often before, only in it for what he can get."

"Stop being so suspicious," Sarah told him. "What can he possibly get out of Mr. Norton? Come on, let's lock up. I'm starving, and you promised to cook supper."

Chapter Six

The opening night of the play was only ten days away, and Miss Timmins was engaged in an orgy of prop gathering. Anybody with a serviceable item was commanded to hand it over on pain of being accused of having no sense of the fitness of things. She dispatched Justin from one end of the village to the other and back, "like a sergeant major," he protested.

The one thing that eluded her ingenuity was a magnificent ball gown for Sarah to wear. It was supposed to represent Amy's flowering to beauty, but Sarah had resigned herself to wearing something bought at a jumble sale and made over.

Strangely enough, it was Imelda who solved the problem. She didn't normally deign to patronize Mottson's, but when she did she managed to enter in such a way that even the doorbell sounded different. She arrived while Sarah was going over the books with Uncle Nick, and Justin was entertaining Nicky.

"Can I help you?" Sarah asked politely.

Imelda produced her most gracious smile. "It is *I* who have come to help *you*," she declared. "I understand that Miss Timmins is collecting props for your latest little show and that there was some difficulty in obtaining a ball gown."

"We're having trouble finding something nice enough," Sarah admitted.

"Then I have the answer." Imelda laid a long box on the counter and lifted from it an ivory satin gown. The bodice was decorated with glittering beads, and the wide skirt flowed dramatically.

Sarah gasped with delight. "It's beautiful. Thank you so much. How generous of you!"

"One likes to do one's duty by the community," Imelda announced sweetly.

"We'll return it in good condition," Sarah promised. "You must love wearing such a beautiful creation."

"Oh, well—I could hardly wear it again, could I?"

Sarah reddened. She was good-natured to a fault, but there was no missing the implication of Imelda's words.

"But I do want it back," the older woman continued. "I wore it at a ball at which royalty was present, so it will form part of the family's heritage collection. I brought it to you because I could hardly approach Miss Timmins."

"Oh, dear. Are you and she at odds again?"

"Not again," Imelda said frostily. "Still. That disgusting tom of hers simply will not learn his place. He's always hanging about Princess Delphine, and it takes all my efforts to avert a misalliance.'' Imelda's eyes were hard. ''Such a thing must not happen. I will not allow it.''

''Perhaps Crosspatch isn't as interested as you think,'' Sarah suggested. ''Maybe Princess Delphine doesn't attract him.''

Imelda gave a tinkly laugh. ''That's absurd! Hoi polloi is always attracted by class. Class must protect itself.''

The two women faced each other, each knowing they weren't talking about cats.

''That woman!'' Nick said with loathing when Imelda had departed. ''I'd just like to get her to myself on a dark night.''

''It wouldn't work,'' Sarah said mischievously. She'd recovered her sense of humor. ''We're hoi polloi. She's class. Class would probably protect itself with a sharp knee.''

''I wasn't thinking of making advances,'' Nick growled. ''More like murder. You know why she did it, don't you?''

''To warn me off,'' Sarah said with a chuckle, ''in case I had any ideas about allying myself to class.''

''How can you laugh about it?'' Justin demanded.

''I can't help finding Mrs. Drew funny. Royalty was present, no less. Just so that I know the Drews are the crème de la crème.''

''Imelda Drew's crème went sour years ago,'' Nick fulminated.

"And the funniest thing of all is the idea that I might be chasing her son."

"You should have thrown her dress back at her," Justin insisted.

"She'd have told the others, and how would I have explained it?"

As if to prove her right, Miss Timmins came in at that moment. The story was soon told, and she bore the box away in triumph after giving Justin a long list of last-minute items that would take him at least a day to get through.

The result was that he was late back the next night and missed the rehearsal. It was a difficult evening. Time was running short, and tempers frayed. Alex arrived the worse for wear, and his eyes lit up when he realized Sarah was alone. She avoided him as much as possible, but when she came offstage he was always waiting for her.

"Mom told me about her dress," he confided, breathing brandy fumes over her.

"It was very kind of her," Sarah said.

He touched her arm. "It's a real sexy number—low cut—can't wait to see you in it, Sarah."

She flinched away from him.

"C'mon, darling, don't give me the cold shoulder. I know you're not really like that."

"Don't call me darling, and you don't know what I'm like."

"I know you've got a little bastard back home, which means you're no blushing violet. Someone's had what you've got to offer, so why not me?"

She turned angry, astonished eyes on him, but Lu-

cinda's voice calling her spared her the necessity of
saying anything. After that she managed to avoid being alone with him, but she was shaken by the reve-
lation of his ugly thoughts. Was that how they saw
her in Haven? She knew it was an old-fashioned place,
and some of her neighbors regarded her as an oddity,
but they were kindhearted, and if they disapproved
they kept it to themselves. She became so distracted
with her troubled thoughts that she forgot her lines
twice.

She was relieved when it was time to go, and
slipped away through the side door. But Alex was
waiting for her outside, blocking her way.

"Let me pass, Alex."

"In a minute. Why don't you come and have a
drink with me?"

"I've got to get home. Please let me pass."

He put his hands on either side of her head, pressing
her against the wall with his body. "Just a kiss—one
little kiss."

"I said no." She tried to push him away, but he
pressed harder, groping tipsily for her breasts.

"You were giving me the come-on in there."

"I wasn't."

"Don't try to deny it."

He seized her head in both hands and forced a
boozy kiss onto her. Sarah rarely lost her temper, but
she lost it now, fighting him off hard enough to force
him back. She hardly recognized Alex. The sunny,
good-tempered boy was gone. Instead his face showed
fury at being denied what he wanted and a drunken
determination to have his way at all costs.

"You little bitch," he spat. "Who the hell do you think you are?"

He slammed her against the wall. Sarah managed to get her arm up across her chest, which infuriated him still more. He wrenched at her shirt, tearing it half-away. She tried to cry out for help, but she was breathless from the struggle and Alex's weight was pressing against her. She kicked and fought as well as she could and could sense that her strength came as an unwelcome surprise to him, but it only served to heighten his anger at being frustrated.

"What game d'you think you're playing?" he demanded through gritted teeth. "You were sending out all the signals. Think I can't tell?"

An angry voice spoke out of the shadows. "That's *just* what I think."

To Sarah's overwhelming relief the voice belonged to Justin. He appeared behind Alex with alarming suddenness, pulled him off, slapped his face and gripped him by the ear. "I think you can't tell when a lady's saying no, because no one ever said that to you in your whole spoilt life," he snapped.

Alex swore at him. He was squirming helplessly, but Justin's hold on his ear was remorseless. "Perhaps if I take you home like this, along the High Street so that everyone can see, you'll learn that no means no," Justin said, as though seriously considering the matter.

Alex gave a yelp of protest and kicked Justin on the shins, just hard enough to make him wince and relax his grip slightly. Alex wriggled free and made a run for it. He got to a safe distance before turning and yelling, "No need to be a dog in the manger."

"And what's that supposed to mean?" Justin demanded grimly.

"You may have squatter's rights now. But you won't stick around forever."

Justin's face darkened with anger. "And then you think Sarah will drop into your hands? Is that it? I have news for you, since you're too fatheaded to understand the signals. The lady doesn't like you."

Alex pulled a small whiskey flask from his pocket and tossed the contents down his throat. It seemed to renew his courage, for he said, "Well, I have news for *you.* That is no lady. That's a hot little number, great for a bit of fun but in no position to be choosy."

By his side Justin heard Sarah's sharp intake of breath at Alex's cruel words.

"I mean, where's the kid's father, eh?" Alex went on. "You don't see him around, do you? She probably doesn't even recall his name, but whoever he is, he didn't want to know about that little bundle."

Dark anger was welling up inside Justin. Alex saw it, and his boozy courage drained away. He backed off, but Justin gave chase, seized his collar and begun to propel him across the green.

"Let me go!" Alex shrieked.

"Not before I've taught you a lesson in manners, you nasty little punk," Justin said through gritted teeth.

Some loiterers on the village green turned at the sight of Justin, holding Alex's collar in one hand and his belt in the other, hauling him across the grass to the duck pond.

"Don't you dare!" Alex roared.

"Who's going to stop me?" Justin demanded. The next moment Alex was flying through the air to land, with a huge splash, in the dark water. Ducks rose into the air, flapping their wings and quacking furiously. Alex surfaced, spluttering and covered with mud.

"You—" he screamed, "you—"

But Justin was already walking away. He went straight to Sarah. "Let's go home," he said, taking her arm gently.

They slipped into the house and up the stairs without attracting Nick's attention. When they were in his room he pulled her against him in a hug. "Don't take any notice of him, Sarah. He doesn't count."

"Yes, I—I know." Her voice trembled, and he held her more tightly, murmuring gentle words against her hair. "I've never seen Alex be like that before," she said. "I knew he could be silly, but he seemed a nice enough boy. Only tonight he was different, nasty. He kept muttering things to me. He thought I was easy, just waiting for him to—"

"What right has he to think you were easy?"

"Because I've got a baby and no sign of his father."

"Damn him! How dare he judge you! He ought to be kicked from here to kingdom come."

She gave a shaky laugh and raised her head to look at him. "Well, you did that, didn't you?" The words died at something she saw in his face.

Justin lowered his head slowly until their lips were barely touching. He whispered her name, and she felt herself melting with happiness. This was what she wanted. Him. Only him. This was why she could never belong to any other man.

He tightened his arms, covering her mouth with his own, kissing her hungrily, and she responded with equal ardor. But in the same moment Justin tensed. Sarah felt his whole body grow stiff, and the next instant he tore himself away from her.

"Justin, what is it?"

He went to stand at the window, looking out at the moonlit scene. He was shaking with the force of the passion he was fighting down, but not for the world would he have hurt her. And it had dawned on him with horrible clarity that after what had happened tonight his very ardor might seem an insult.

"Don't you want me?" she asked softly.

With a groan he turned to her. "You know how much I want you," he said raggedly. "I want to make love with you right now, but I can't, unless—"

"Unless what?"

"Unless you tell me that you know I'm not like Alex Drew, thinking you easy and out for what I can get."

"Justin, I've never thought that."

"Are you sure? Isn't that the real reason?"

"I don't understand. The reason for what?"

"The barrier between us. Because there *is* one, Sarah. You know there is. Even when we seem closest I can feel the shadow of something, or someone, that you can't forget. Is it that you don't trust me?"

"No, no," she said earnestly.

"Or don't you trust any man—because of Nicky's

PLAY SILHOUETTE'S

LUCKY HEARTS

GAME

AND YOU GET

- ♦ **FREE BOOKS!**
- ♦ **A FREE GIFT!**
- ♦ **AND MUCH MORE!**

TURN THE PAGE AND DEAL YOURSELF IN...

Play "Lucky Hearts" and you get.

YOURS FREE!

This lovely necklace will add glamour to your most elegant outfit! Its cobra-link chain is a generous 18" long, and its lustrous simulated cultured pearl is mounted in an attractive pendant! Best of all, it's ABSOLUTELY FREE, just for accepting our NO-RISK offer.

...then continue your lucky streak with a sweetheart of a deal!

1. Play Lucky Hearts as instructed on the opposite page.
2. Send back this card and you'll receive brand-new Silhouette Special Edition® novels. These books have a cover price of $3.99 each, but they are yours to keep absolutely free.
3. There's no catch. You're under no obligation to buy anything. We charge nothing— ZERO—for your first shipment. And you don't have to make any minimum number of purchases—not even one!
4. The fact is thousands of readers enjoy receiving books by mail from the Silhouette Reader Service™. They like the convenience of home delivery...they like getting the best new novels BEFORE they're available in stores...and they love our discount prices!
5. We hope that after receiving your free books you'll want to remain a subscriber. But the choice is yours—to continue or cancel, any time at all! So why not take us up on our invitation, with no risk of any kind. You'll be glad you did!

©1996 HARLEQUIN ENTERPRISES LTD.

◆ **Exciting Silhouette romance novels—FREE!**

◆ **Plus a lovely Simulated Pearl Drop Necklace—FREE!**

DETACH AND MAIL CARD TODAY!

YES!

I have scratched off the silver card. Please send me all the free books and gift for which I qualify. I understand that I am under no obligation to purchase any books, as explained on the back and on the opposite page.

With a coin, scratch off the silver card and check below to see what we have for you.

235 CIS CA7W (U-SIL-SE-07/97)

SILHOUETTE'S

LUCKY HEARTS

GAME

NAME

ADDRESS _____ APT.

CITY _____ STATE _____ ZIP

Twenty-one gets you 4 free books, and a free Simulated Pearl Drop Necklace!

Twenty gets you 4 free books!

Nineteen gets you 3 free books!

Eighteen gets you 2 free books!

Offer limited to one per household and not valid to current Silhouette Special Edition® subscribers. All orders subject to approval.

PRINTED IN U.S.A.

The Silhouette Reader Service™—Here's how it works:

Accepting free books places you under no obligation to buy anything. You may keep the books and gift and return the shipping statement marked "cancel." If you do not cancel, about a month later we'll send you 6 additional novels and bill you just $3.34 each plus 25¢ delivery per book and applicable sales tax, if any.* That's the complete price—and compared to cover prices of $3.99 each—quite a bargain! You may cancel any time, but if you choose to continue, every month we'll send you 6 more books, which you may either purchase at the discount price...or return to us and cancel your subscription.
*Terms and prices subject to change without notice. Sales tax applicable in N.Y.

If offer card is missing write to: Silhouette Reader Service, 3010 Walden Ave., P.O. Box 1867, Buffalo, NY 14240-1867

SILHOUETTE READER SERVICE
3010 WALDEN AVE
PO BOX 1867
BUFFALO NY 14240-9952

BUSINESS REPLY MAIL
FIRST-CLASS MAIL   PERMIT NO. 717   BUFFALO, NY

POSTAGE WILL BE PAID BY ADDRESSEE

NO POSTAGE
NECESSARY
IF MAILED
IN THE
UNITED STATES

father? Tell me. Don't let me flounder, wondering what I have to do to get it right.''

She touched his lips lightly, first with her fingertips, then with her mouth. "You don't have to do anything," she whispered, "except this."

"Yes," he murmured against her mouth.

"Just this, and this..."

He gathered her to him in one urgent, hungry movement. His fears fell away as he felt the sweet ardor of her body responding to his passion. He kissed her mouth, her eyes, touching her with reverence, trying to show by tenderness what she meant to him.

Sarah felt herself drowning in the pleasure of the long, slow kiss he gave her, his mouth moving over hers with leisurely ease. His tongue slid between her lips and found its place naturally, exploring the inside of her mouth with feather-light strokes. Each little flickering movement heightened her sensations, making her long for the inevitable conclusion. But Justin wasn't to be hurried.

"How dare he lay a finger on you," he murmured. "He knows nothing about you. He doesn't see you as I do—"

"Forget Alex," she said. "You said yourself he doesn't count. Nothing else counts while we have this."

He covered her mouth again and began to explore more deeply. The hard length of his body was pressed against hers, and even through their clothes she could feel his rising tide of need. She trembled pleasurably at the thought of the encounter to come.

His wandering hands discovered the torn shirt and

began to remove it, revealing faint bruises on the skin beneath. He swore softly before laying gentle lips against them, driving pain away with the tenderness of his love.

"I should have done a lot more than toss him in the duck pond," he said huskily.

"Never mind. It's over now. Love me, Justin."

He threw off his clothes and helped her with the last of hers. Instead of taking her straight to bed he sat on the edge and drew her between his knees so he could wrap his arms around her, laying his head against her breast. She stroked his hair and rested her cheek against him.

His fingers outlined her curves, touching her softly, intimately, in ways that she loved. His tongue was teasing one peaked nipple, circling it with small rasping movements that heightened her excitement. It felt so wonderful, pure ravishing delight streaming through her body, out to her fingers and toes.

He felt the change in her breathing and quickly drew her down onto the bed beside him. He was a skilled lover. He knew how to excite a woman and bring her physical release. His controlled technique was a weapon, along with many others, contributing to his reputation as a man who succeeded at everything.

But tonight he forgot about weapons and success. He was making love, his body obeying the impulses of his heart and soul. Sarah sensed it in every caress, and her body relaxed as it became more intimately his. She touched him in wonder, feeling the leashed power behind the restraint.

He pulled back to look at her face, and something in her smile seemed to reassure him. When Sarah reached out to him he instantly took her hand, pressing it against his mouth and stroking the palm with his tongue. It felt good, but her feverish body was beyond light caresses. She craved him deeply, primitively, and now.

"Justin, I want you," she whispered.

"Are you sure, Sarah? Is this really what you want?"

For answer she gripped his shoulders and pulled him over her in a fever of impatience. To her incredulous delight he laughed, something he'd never been relaxed enough to do in the past.

"I guess you're sure," he said.

Once he knew how much she desired him he wasted no time, entering her quickly, so that she gasped with the pleasure. She wrapped her legs around his hips, telling him silently what she wanted, and felt his powerful reaction deep within her. She was lost in the profound depths of her sensuality, giving back passion for passion with a hot urgency that removed the last of his caution. He claimed her like a man possessed, dazzled by the beauty she offered. The fierce magic consumed them both, merging them into one creature, both loved and loving, giving and taking.

It was she who urged them on to their climax, driving against him. He responded vigorously, thrusting deep inside her, giving her his all in powerful movements of hips and thighs until their final moment of explosive release. But when the moment was past he only held her more firmly, like a man who'd discovered a secret and feared to let it slip away.

They lay quiet for a while, then she heard him chuckle. "What is it?"

"I was thinking of Alex in the duck pond. That was the most fun I've had in years."

She joined in his laughter. "You really enjoyed that," she accused.

"You bet I did."

"Well, maybe I did, too. You were right about Alex. He wasn't the harmless little boy I thought." Her laughter died. "Is that how they really think of me here?"

"You know better than that," he said quickly. "Don't let that lout spoil anything. These are good, kind people. They take folks as they find them. If anyone should know that, it's me."

"You're right," she said contentedly. And the contentment was as much at hearing how he spoke of Haven as anything else.

It was blissful to lie in his arms, feeling the beating of her heart slow down and a drowsy heaviness overtake her limbs. No telephones, no faxes, nothing but their two selves.

"Are you asleep?" he whispered after a while.

"No. I'm so happy I don't want to lose a moment of it."

"I'm glad." But then an impulse he couldn't control made him say, "It's just that I still wish you'd confide in me. There's something standing between us, and I know now it isn't Alex."

"Hush! Don't ask me any more."

"Will you tell me one day?"

"Maybe the time will come when I can tell you— or when you'll understand without being told. I don't know. I hope so."

He waited, hoping she would say more, but she was silent. Justin lay still, trying to come to terms with his jealousy. His brain seethed with questions. *Did you lie like this with him, your head resting against his heart? Did he hold you as I do, listening to the sound of your breathing? Does what we share drive him from your mind, or is it less than you shared with him? Are you thinking of him now?* But he didn't ask these questions, because he was afraid of the answers.

She stirred and began to slide out of bed, but he held her.

"I have to go and check Nicky," she said.

He followed her. Nicky was just opening his eyes. "Can I help?" he asked.

"You can heat up his milk while I change him."

He returned a few minutes later with the milk just right. She already had Nicky settled in the crook of her arm. She took the bottle from him with a smile, tested it for temperature and began to feed her son. Justin watched them, trying not to mind her absorption.

"Is Nicky like his father?" he asked abruptly.

"I'm not sure," she said slowly. She'd known this moment must come. "If you mean, was Nicky's father always laughing and sweet-tempered, no. Not when I met him. But I used to think it would have been nice to have known him when he was young, before the world got to him and he started to believe that only size and money mattered.'' She stopped, unsure how much it was safe to say.

"What was his name?" But Sarah shook her head. "Why not?"

"His name doesn't matter."

"What did you mean about the world getting to him?"

"He'd been born poor, and he'd made his mark in the world by himself. But he'd begun to feel that only the struggle mattered. He'd forgotten about people."

"But you saw something in him."

"I think I saw the man nature meant him to be, fine and generous. He did laugh sometimes, and then..." She stopped with a little smile.

Justin saw it, and his bitterness rose. He wished he could make himself stop this, but he *had* to know about the man who'd taken possession of Sarah's heart. It was incredible that she could still love him, but that smile and the soft, faraway look in her eyes told their own story.

"How did you meet him?" he asked.

Sarah decided to take the risk. "At his firm's party," she said. "He said I didn't look as if I was enjoying myself, and he didn't care for it, either." She stole a glance at Justin to see if her description was touching a chord in his mind, but he gave no sign of it.

"It was only when the speeches began that I realized he was the boss," she continued. "Later he insisted on driving me home. After that we saw each other quite often."

"And you loved him?" Justin forced himself to ask.

"Yes," she said simply. "I loved him with all my heart."

Justin let out a long breath, wondering how anything could hurt so much. There was a note in Sarah's voice that he couldn't bear. It was filled with longing and bittersweet memory, as though her love had been so beautiful she would cherish it forever, even if it meant embracing pain as the price. He felt she'd slipped away into a secret world shared only by herself and this unknown man, while he was outside.

"And then it was over," Sarah said. "I think I knew before he did. We started arguing. One night he said he'd be busy for a while, and he'd call me later. He didn't, of course. I knew he wouldn't."

Justin swore softly, but Sarah shook her head.

"No, why should I call him names just because he didn't feel the same as I did? People can't love to order."

"But they don't have to be fools about it," Justin said. "If he'd won your love he should have thanked heaven, not thrown it away."

Her heart leaped at his words, and even more at his tone. She took hold of the hand with which he was stroking her face and rubbed her cheek against it.

"Did he know about the baby?" Justin asked.

"Yes. I went back to see him. I didn't want him to marry me, not if he didn't want to. But I never dreamed he'd want me to have an abortion." Her voice shook. For a moment she was back in his austere apartment, listening to him reject their child.

"The bastard!" he said softly.

"He meant to do right by me. He was going to pay

for everything—a good clinic, the best care. I'd thought he cared for me a little—not loved me as I did him, but a little. But I was a naive fool. Our child meant nothing to him, just an inconvenience to be gotten rid of. I couldn't bear it. So I ran away."

"Good!" Justin said fervently. "You're better off without him."

"I felt as if he'd destroyed some of the good between us. I had to get well away from him before he spoiled all my memories. I wanted to keep some of my belief in him."

"For God's sake, why?"

"Because he's still Nicky's father."

Nicky grunted in her arms, and Sarah looked down. Justin thought how quickly she forgot him for the child. Every loving glance and smile given to Nicky was also for the man who'd sired him. It made him bitter to think that, after the overwhelming experience they'd just shared, she could be drawn back so quickly to that other love.

He watched for as long as he could bear, then went to his room and locked the door.

There was an aftermath to the incident with Alex. Haven awoke next morning to the news that young Mr. Drew had been called away from the village by urgent family affairs.

"Of course, there is another version," Sergeant Mayhew told Justin when he made his collection. "Some say he was set upon by a dozen thugs."

"Only a dozen?" Justin asked.

"Or more. Supposedly he beat 'em off single-handed."

"I heard they threw him into the duck pond," Justin remarked.

"No, sir, he *fell* into the duck pond when he collapsed after his heroic efforts."

"A giant among men," Justin remarked.

The policeman's face gave nothing away. "As you say, sir. I don't think we'll be seeing him around here for quite a while. Good morning."

When Miss Timmins heard the true story she locked up Imelda's dress and prepared to stand firm against demands for its return. But her care was needless. Imelda had been discouraged from rash action by her seldom seen husband, who pointed out that this would instantly confirm the more undignified rumors about their son. Instead she took refuge in glacial dignity, which fooled nobody. Everyone knew the truth through Mrs. Dakers, who cleaned for Imelda three mornings a week.

Alex's departure left an awkward gap in the ranks of the dramatic society. In the end the juvenile lead doubled up the comic gardener, and Lucinda's seventeen-year-old grandson was press-ganged into playing Frank on pain of having certain peccadillos revealed to his parents.

The production was a triumphant success. The Haven Players had a reputation for miles around, and the three hundred seats were filled for both nights of its run.

Justin worked hard backstage, building scenery, prompting, relaying messages and carrying things. He

was acclaimed as the most efficient assistant stage
manager the Players had ever had. To crown his growing popularity he provided the funds not only for the
opening night party but the closing night party, too,
thus showing, as Miss Timmins observed, a sense of
the fitness of things.

But the next day, trouble struck. Miss Timmins,
gathering props to return them to their rightful owners,
discovered that Mrs. Drew's royal dress was missing.
Everyone conducted a frantic search, but despite their
attempts at secrecy it came to Imelda's ears. Things
might have gotten even nastier but for a disaffected
member of Joker's gang, who revealed that his leader
was the culprit. Sarah, who was present to hear this,
ran home to find Justin.

"You've got to come," she said breathlessly. "Mrs.
Drew's on the warpath, and Joker's already been in
trouble with the police."

It was late evening. The store was closed, and Nick
was just about to set off for the Haystack, but he readily agreed to stay at home with the baby while the
other two went. "But I want the whole scandal as soon
as possible," he called after them.

They reached the poky little house where Joker
lived with his widowed mother, arriving just as the
dress was discovered hidden in a plastic bag under the
boy's bed.

In vain Joker protested he'd never meant to keep
his plunder. It had served its purpose, and he was looking for a way to return it. "I was gonna get it back
next day, but Ma Timmins found it missing first."

"A likely story," Imelda said, sniffing. "This is a matter for the law."

"Hang on." Justin stopped her. "Joker, just what was its purpose?"

A grin broke over Joker's face. "These," he said.

Before a riveted audience he produced a wallet of photographs fresh from being developed and handed them around. Imelda shrieked. The others regarded the pictures in stunned silence, shielding their twitching lips with their hands.

Imelda's royal gown had been lovingly draped over Timmy Bags.

"A scarecrow!" Imelda exploded. "You put my dress on a scarecrow!"

"It ain't hurt," Joker protested.

"Vandal! Thief!"

"He's not a thief," Justin objected. "He was going to give it back."

"So he says. We found it in his possession. That's theft. You've been in trouble before, my lad. Well, it'll be the reformatory for you this time."

There was an outcry. Sarah put her arms about Joker's weeping mother. "Justin, do something," she pleaded.

"There's no need to take it that far," Justin said. "This was a prank. He'd have put it back—"

"I might have known *you'd* stand up for this ruffian," Imelda snapped.

"Nonsense, he's just a lad with a lot of energy and imagination, and not enough for them to do. In fact he's the sort of—" Justin stopped, on the verge of saying Joker might be the sort of raw material his firm needed. "The sort I was myself once," he amended.

"He's a criminal," Imelda insisted.

"He's not a criminal, but he soon will be if you make a fuss about a practical joke," Justin said. "I'm asking you to give him another chance. Aren't we all entitled to another chance?"

Watching his face, Sarah was puzzled to see a strange look come over it. For a moment he was confused. Then it passed, and he became Justin Hallwood again, a man used to command and, if necessary, intrigue to get his way.

He placed himself in front of Imelda. "Mrs. Drew, I'll make a deal with you," he said. "You take your dress home and say nothing of this to the police, and I'll make sure that none of those pictures fall into the wrong hands."

"I've got them here," she snapped, holding up the wallet. "They'll be burnt as soon as I reach home."

Justin paused before delivering his bombshell. "What about the others?"

"Others?"

"You don't think this is the only set of prints, do you? Joker's a resourceful lad. There must be at least one other set, which I will undertake to find and destroy."

There was a silence, in which everyone present imagined Joker scattering his pictures far and wide. Imelda clearly imagined it, too, for she blanched. Her blazing, spiteful eyes met Justin's cool, determined ones. Her eyes fell first.

"Can you guarantee you'll get every print?"

"Every last one," Justin said, with a look at Joker that boded ill if there was trouble.

"Naturally, one wishes to show compassion," Imelda said, going into regal mode.

"I was sure we could rely on you," Justin said smoothly.

When Mrs. Drew had departed he shooed the rest away. "Joker and I have some talking to do," he said.

To Sarah's eyes he still looked very pale, as though his moment's confusion had left a strain he hadn't confronted yet. But he gave her a smile as he ushered her out.

"Now," he said to Joker when he'd closed the door, "the others."

Grinning, Joker produced another set from under his mattress.

"And the rest," Justin said.

"Aw, c'mon."

"The rest."

Joker rummaged in the back of a drawer and produced another wallet. Justin glanced through it, then looked up, raising his eyebrows significantly. After a silent battle of wills Joker scrabbled under his bed for the pictures he'd carefully stored in a separate place.

"Blowed how you knew," he grumbled.

"Been there. Done it," Justin informed him. "Is this the lot?"

"Word of honor."

"All right. I'll accept your word of honor. If you break it I won't bother with the police, I'll personally make you sorry you were born."

Joker nodded, clearly finding this reasonable.

Justin wandered to the store, so thoughtful he'd walked past it and almost into the duck pond before he realized what he was doing. Sarah was watching for him at the window.

"Is it all right?" she asked anxiously. He told her what had happened. "How did you know what he'd have done?" she asked.

"Because I saw myself in him. I was a handful at that age. Mostly innocent stuff, but I might have gone to the bad if someone hadn't taken me in hand. It was the vicar. He almost twisted my arm to get me into engineering college."

"Was that why you had that faraway look on your face when you were talking about a second chance?"

"No, that was…something else. Sarah, I had the weirdest sensation, as though what was happening ought to be familiar."

"Because you saw yourself in Joker?"

"No, it was to do with the last two years. When I said a second chance, the air was singing. I was on the edge of remembering…. It was there, almost within my grasp, and it was important. That's what I'm trying to recall—someone who should have been given a second chance, but they weren't, and everything went wrong after that. Dear God," he shouted in frustration.

"What did I do?" he asked desperately. "I treated someone unkindly, I wouldn't let them make amends, pride—damnable pride—wanting to hurt someone like they'd hurt me—hell, I don't know. Sarah, what's the matter?" He'd looked up to find her staring at him with a wild, horrified look. "Darling, what is it?"

"Justin, suppose it's the other way around. Suppose

it's someone who wouldn't give *you* a second chance?''

"I don't think that's likely."

"But you don't know."

"I know the sort of man I've always been, and I never asked anyone to let me off. It's not my way. No, it's me." He sighed. "But it's no use trying to remember it. Trying just drives it away. I guess I'll go to bed. Maybe it'll come back while I'm asleep. Although frankly, I'm beginning to lose hope."

He kissed her cheek and departed, unhappily.

Nick arrived home merry after consuming a liter of cider and trouncing Colly at chess. But his smile faded when he saw Sarah on the sofa in the darkness and realized that she was weeping. "Hey, what's this?" he asked, alarmed.

Sarah hastily dabbed her eyes. "I'm fine, honestly. No, don't put the light on. I've just been having a think."

"And that made you cry?"

"I've realized that I did something terrible. I didn't understand, but I was so wrong. I did Justin a dreadful injury."

"Hmph! It seems to me like he did you the injury. Didn't he abandon you when you were pregnant?"

"Not really. I saw it all tonight, when he was talking about second chances. He thinks he didn't give someone another chance when they needed it, but it wasn't him, it was *me*."

"But he tried to force you to have an abortion."

"No, not force—he said it in the heat of the moment, but he couldn't have forced me, and I know he wouldn't have tried. I think I could have made him accept that my mind was made up. And then he'd have come to visit Nicky because he'd have been curious about *his* baby. I see now what Nicky would have done for him, how he'd have taught him about love. And I denied him that—out of pride.''

"A bit more than pride, surely?''

"No, it was pride,'' Sarah said with self-condemning bitterness. "Damnable pride. I took him by surprise, and when he didn't react as I wanted I said something so cruel I can't even tell you about it. And then I vanished. I wouldn't let him find me and make it right. If I'd given him another chance I'm sure he'd have made use of it. But I didn't. Oh, Uncle Nick, don't you see? He didn't abandon me. *I* abandoned *him.*''

"Don't be so set on taking the blame, darling.''

"Perhaps I should have blamed myself a little more and him a little less. I might have spared him this.''

"Would that have been a good thing?'' Uncle Nick asked shrewdly. "He needed to learn for himself what was important, and he mightn't have done that if you'd made it too easy.''

She knew there was a lot of sense in Nick's words, but it still hurt her to see Justin so troubled. She bade the old man good-night and went to her room.

Nicky was sleeping peacefully. She kissed him softly, not to awaken him. She was bewildered, wondering what the future held and what she should do for the best, and her heart ached for the man she loved.

There was a light tap on her door. Justin stood there.

"Is everything all right, Sarah?''

"Yes," she said huskily. "I'm fine."

But he heard a note in her voice that worried him. "What is it?" he asked urgently, shutting the door behind him. "Have you been crying?"

"It's just—I'm tired, and it's been a long day."

"Tell me what's upset you," he insisted half-angrily. "I've got the right to know. No." He checked himself hastily. "Not right. I didn't mean that. But I want to know what's in your heart. What about *him?*" he demanded jealously. "Would you have told him?"

"I don't think he'd ever have asked. He didn't notice things as you do. Let it go for now, Justin. One day you'll understand—and then perhaps you'll forgive me."

"Forgive you?" The words startled him. "You could never do anything I'd need to forgive. I don't believe you've ever done an unkind act or thought an unkind thought in your life."

"Don't think too well of me. If you only knew..."

"I know *you,*" he said simply. "And that's all I need to know. Good night, my darling."

Chapter Seven

The only small cloud in Sarah's sky was the problem of finding time to be alone with Justin. Oddly enough, it was Nick who solved it. Sarah came into the kitchen one morning to find him just replacing the phone.

"That was your uncle Joe," he said. "He and Ethel booked a vacation in a seaside caravan, but she's got a funny tummy, so they're going home early. The van's paid for until the end of the week, and we can have the last three days if we like."

"It sounds lovely, but how can we leave the shop at short notice?" Sarah asked wistfully.

"You can if I stay here," the old man said. "You and Justin. I'll look after Nicky. It'll be just you two." He gave her a sly wink.

Sarah threw her arms around his neck. "You do like him, don't you?" she asked gleefully.

"Well, I will say he went up in my estimation when I saw him taking Mrs. Timmins's orders with never a word of complaint." He assumed a falsetto voice. "'Do this, do that, hurry up, young man, we haven't got all day.' And him saying, 'Yes ma'am, no ma'am,' as meek as a baby. But I don't think he's a meek man normally."

"He certainly isn't!"

"So why was he doing it?"

"To help the Haven Players," Sarah said primly, but her eyes were dancing.

"Hmm! Put it that way if you like. He's sure trying to get into *someone's* good books."

Justin arrived a moment later, was told of the plan and immediately endorsed it. But with a condition. "I'm hiring a car in Market Dorsey to take us there," he said. "You say this place is only ten miles away, but..." He paused tactfully while Nick bridled.

"You were going to say something about my car?" he demanded.

"I was going to say we can't deprive you of it," Justin continued smoothly, and shushed Sarah out of the side of his mouth when she giggled.

He got the bus to Market Dorsey and returned driving a car that had been carefully chosen from the middle of the range. It offered a smoother ride than Nick's bone shaker—but then, what car didn't?—without marking him out as a rich man.

The weather was broiling hot, and the caravan site, on the edge of the beach, was a welcome sight. The site manager showed them to their van, which was large and comfortable, told them where to find some shops and departed with Justin's tip.

After Sarah called home to reassure herself about Nicky, they shopped, stocking up on food, buying swimming trunks for Justin, then hurried back to change for a swim. A few moments later they were plunging into the sparkling water, gasping at its chilly impact on their skins and splashing each other like children. They raced, and he was chagrined to find that it took him an effort to beat her. She had the strength of a countrywoman, and he still wasn't at his best.

A motorboat came by, slowing so the driver could shout at them, "Go back. There's a dangerous undertow beyond here. People have been drowned. The council ought to set up warning signs, but they won't in case it damages trade."

They thanked him and swam to shore. In the evening they visited the funfair and tried everything, clutching each other on the ghost train, laughing at their distorted images in the hall of mirrors and eating toffee apples. Justin tried a rifle stall and won a fat, furry gorilla for Nicky.

"And it only took you thirty attempts," Sarah teased him. "You could have bought it for half that."

He did better at the next stall, winning a tiny bear at the first try and solemnly presenting her with it.

"What shall we do now?" he asked. "Go out for a meal or go home and make love?"

Sarah sighed and clutched her stomach. "I'm simply *starving,*" she declared.

"So am I—but not for food."

"I'm starving for food," she insisted, looking at him innocently.

But he was a man of action. And he took it.

"Justin, put me down. There are people watching. *Put me down!*"

He did, but not until they were inside the caravan, when he deposited her on the bed and locked the door.

"What about my supper?"

"Afterward," he said firmly, beginning to undress her. "Afterward."

They made love in a riot of joy. Then he cooked the supper, but they only got halfway through before being distracted. They were too weary to eat after that, and fell asleep in each other's arms.

The three days they spent in Barton were so happy as to seem almost unreal. After the long time spent parched of Justin's love, Sarah found herself bathed in it, reveling in it. Surely now, she thought, she might risk telling him the truth? She began to plot her moment, waiting for a natural opening. Perhaps it would happen at night, when they'd fulfilled each other and were resting in peace and contentment. On their second night in Barton she was lying with her head against his, relaxing from the pleasure of love, when Justin spoke quietly above her head.

"I wish I'd met you earlier in my life."

Sarah's heart almost stopped. "Why?" she asked breathlessly.

"You'd have been good for me. I might have liked myself better now."

"You don't know what you're like now."

"Not from memory, but I can read the signs in the

paperwork of the past two years. People I put out of business, took advantage of. It wasn't a nice man who did that. He was hard and cruel—"

"Not cruel," she said at once, and caught herself quickly. "I mean, I don't believe you could ever be cruel."

"I hope you go on thinking so. Perhaps it's as well you didn't know me then. You'd have hated me, and I couldn't bear that."

"I could never have hated you," Sarah said. "It might have been painful to love you, but I'd have done it anyway."

"Then you might have stopped me going wrong."

"Don't be so hard on yourself," she said softly. "What you are now is what you were then. The good and the kindness were always there."

"But it took you to bring them out." He sighed. "Why couldn't you have come into my life sooner? Where were you when I needed you, Sarah?" Then he tensed. "Ah, yes. I was forgetting. You were in love with someone else."

She said nothing, hoping he wouldn't pursue the subject. She knew her plan of telling him the truth would have to wait.

"I wonder what would have happened if we'd met then," Justin mused. "You'd have been with him, and I'd have liked to meet him face to face and see what kind of a swine won your heart. I can't say I admire your taste." There was a bitter note in his voice. The harmony that had united them a few minutes ago was fractured.

Justin knew it would be wiser to keep quiet, but he

couldn't help himself. The imp of jealousy, which he usually stifled, had leaped on him while he lay with Sarah in his arms, reminding him that her heart held another loyalty.

If she'd been a different sort of woman it would have mattered less. If Nicky had resulted from a casual affair, Justin knew he could have lived with it more easily. But Sarah wasn't the woman to indulge in casual affairs. When she loved she gave all of herself, heart and soul as well as body, and it was that all he resented, feeling as if someone had stolen a gift reserved for him.

He knew he should stop now, but the imp was at work, tearing him, driving him to make her miserable, too.

"Was he anything like me?" he asked in a light voice to disguise his real feelings.

"Justin, stop this," she said desperately. "It's over. Please forget it."

"How can I forget him when you can't? Whatever you feel for me, I don't think you've stopped loving him."

It would have been so easy to tell him what he wanted to hear, that her love for Nicky's father was dead. But one day he would remember everything, including what she said now. "I can't forget," she said at last. "But I love you."

"You love me, you love him. It's getting damned crowded in here!"

He rose abruptly, pulled on some shorts and left the caravan. It was night but the moon was brilliant, bathing the shore and the sea in silver. Justin ran barefoot along the edge of the water, going faster and faster, trying to leave behind the thoughts that hounded him. But they pursued him, snapping at his heels, and when at last he slowed for breath they were still there.

He sat on a rock and buried his head in his hands, trying not to see the images behind his eyes. They'd been there since he'd heard how her lover had received the news of their child. It was like a scene on film that played over and over. He knew exactly how Sarah would have looked, her face radiant with the glory of life and love, then distraught at the brutal rejection. The man was in shadow, but Justin didn't need to see his face to hate him. From Sarah's words he knew the kind of man he was, cold, efficient, incapable of love.

"You bastard!" he muttered. "Oh, you rotten bastard! Why can't I have you here now, for just five minutes?"

He couldn't keep still. Only movement gave him release. He headed for the sea, plunging into the chilly waves and stroking strongly out to the horizon. He swam until he was tired and rested to catch his breath before heading to shore. But then he felt the yank of the current at his feet, and realized he'd come out beyond the safety point.

Horrified, he saw how much distance lay between him and the shore. Already tired, he must fight his way against the undertow that was insistently trying to haul him out to sea. Already, simply treading water, he'd been drawn out a good twenty feet.

He began to swim to the shore, forcing his weary limbs into greater efforts. The current fought him every inch of the way, tugging at his feet like a determined enemy. It was fatal to stop for breath. He plowed on blindly and at last realized with relief that the current had died away. He'd reached the safety area, but was still some distance from the shore, and he was exhausted.

He paused to tread water, taking deep breaths, trying to will himself to the last effort. Then he heard his name echoing across the water.

"Justin!"

It was Sarah's voice. He could make out her tiny figure on the shore, calling him frantically. He raised an arm to wave and immediately went under. He surfaced, gasping, his eyes filled with water. For a dreadful moment he couldn't tell which way he was going. Then her voice came again, pinpointing the shore, guiding him home. Using all his strength, he forced himself on, and at last felt the blessed firmness of sand beneath his feet. He tried to stand but his legs gave way. Then Sarah was there beside him, pulling his arm around her shoulders, supporting him the last few steps. At the edge of the water his legs went again, but she gripped him tightly, refusing to let him fall. "You're not lying down until we're well clear," she said, in a more commanding voice than he'd ever heard her use.

At last she released him, and he sprawled on the dry sand, breathing hard. He couldn't open his eyes, his head ached, and there was singing in his ears, but he was conscious enough to hear Sarah.

"Justin, look at me, *please*. Oh, God, I can't bear this. I can't lose you again, I *can't*."

"It's all right," he managed to gasp, "I'm not dead—be fine in a minute—"

"You idiot!" she breathed. "You idiot. How dare you do such a stupid thing?"

That made him open his eyes. Sarah's face was frantic, the tears pouring down her cheeks. "I'm all right, honestly," he said in a voice that was hoarse from sea water. "If you'll help me I can make it back to the caravan."

He had to lean on her all the way, and collapsed again onto the bed. He resisted her attempts to call an ambulance, even going so far as to hide the mobile phone and threaten her with retribution if she went out to call, although he'd begun to realize that under her quiet ways was a core of no-nonsense strength he hadn't discovered before.

"Fancy you bawling me out," he said, sitting up in bed to eat the soup she'd heated for him. "I've never heard you like that before. What happened to my gentle Sarah?"

"She stops being gentle when people do daft things," she said firmly. "What's more, the next time you pull such a stupid stunt, your gentle Sarah is going to kick your shins."

He grinned. "That's my girl!"

"Now, eat the fish I've cooked for you."

"I'm not sure—"

"Eat it."

"Yes, ma'am."

She didn't take her eyes off him until he'd obeyed, and he had to admit he felt better for the hot food.

"What possessed you to swim out that far?"

"I was trying to outrun my jealousy. But I know now that's not the way." He took her hand. "I'm sorry for what I said tonight."

"You have nothing to be jealous of."

"You don't now how I feel about you, Sarah. I don't just want your love. I want everything about you, not merely what this man left over, but everything." His voice became wry. "Couldn't you at least pretend to hate him, just to make me feel better?"

"Is that what you want from me? Pretense?"

He shook his head. "No, I want only what you *are*, good and honest, incapable of mean or petty thought. I guess I'll have to learn to think my way around this."

When he was half-asleep he remembered wondering what Sarah had meant by, "I can't lose you again." But then he realized she must have been referring to the time he walked away from Haven.

That was the only incident that marred their time at Barton. When the moment came to leave they both looked around the caravan, trying to imprint it on their minds. There was an ache of regret in Sarah's heart that only the thought of seeing Nicky again could assuage.

Her reunion with her son was everything she'd hoped. He bounced around in her arms and squeezed her until she gasped. Justin, too, got an eager greeting. He hugged the little boy, wondering who, if anyone, had ever welcomed him so warmly before. He presented the gorilla, which was warmly received, and tried to teach Nicky the word. But all Nicky could manage was "Ger—ger," and his new friend was called Ger from that moment.

Sarah wanted to spend some time with Nicky to make up for her absence, and Uncle Nick wanted to resume his feud with Colly. It was noticeable that on the days when they didn't trade insults both men seemed to wilt a little.

The Haven Players didn't meet in the summer, so when Sarah and Justin had been back a week they deposited the baby with the Graingers and took Uncle Nick to the Haystack.

But as soon as they entered the pub they could see that something was wrong. The air seemed to hum with indignation. Brenda stood in the corner of a small crowd, talking furiously.

"I don't believe it," Miss Timmins was saying, pink-cheeked. "You must have misunderstood, Brenda, dear. Nobody could do such a wicked thing."

"There's no misunderstanding." Colly stoutly defended his granddaughter. "I saw it myself in black and white."

"But they can't do it," Ted roared. "It'll destroy Haven."

"What's happened?" Sarah asked anxiously.

"They're going to develop Haven," Brenda said. "There's going to be a shopping complex on the green and blocks of high-rise flats over the fields behind. I was talking to someone on the *County Advertiser* today, and he says it's all settled."

"It can't be," Ted insisted. "That land belongs to the village."

"The parish council is selling it," Brenda said, almost in tears.

"Councillor Norton!" Sarah exclaimed. "That's what he meant when he said Haven's time had come. Oh, how could he?"

"Has the sale actually gone through?" Justin demanded.

"All but," Brenda told him. "There's going to be an announcement any day. Look, my contact gave me a copy of the plan." She held out a sheet of paper, and Justin studied it. It showed development all over the green, where the hall now stood and onto the fields in the rear. Some apartment blocks had been indicated, but they were crowded to one side, like an afterthought.

"The official line is that the development will be a fine thing because people need houses," Brenda said. "But it seems to me the real point is the shopping complex."

"Brenda, did you get the name of the company?" Justin demanded.

"Yes, it was D and S. I've never heard of it."

"I have," he said quietly. "It's a powerful firm, and it gets what it wants."

Sarah was watching him with the eyes of love that noticed every detail. She saw that whatever he knew about this company had given him a vision of what was to come. She saw, too, that his old and new selves were facing each other uneasily, the one applauding a shrewd money-making deal, the other...

Abruptly Justin turned and went out, striding over the crossroads to the green. The others followed. He was still a stranger among them, yet he was so purposeful it seemed natural to follow his lead.

Summer was at its height, and there was still enough evening light for Justin to look around and see what the company had in mind.

"How can anyone be so wicked as to want to spoil this place?" Brenda demanded. "Why here, when there are so many better places?"

"Actually there aren't," Justin said, with sudden realization. "Now we know what they have in mind, it's obvious that Haven's perfect. It's an axis, with roads radiating in four directions to surrounding towns. The space is here—the green, the fields stretching behind it. Room for a shopping complex and a parking lot. Money will pour into Haven."

"But Haven would no longer exist," Sarah said passionately. She couldn't believe Justin was talking like this. "The village will be buried alive under this development."

"We need the hall," someone cried. "What can we do?"

"Nothing," Ted shouted. "The big boys have stitched us up. By God, I'll have Norton's head for this. He should have warned us."

"He didn't want to warn us," Sarah said. "He's delighted with all this because it makes him feel important. But it'll ruin Haven." She had her eyes on Justin. If only he would say something to prove her fears were wrong. But he'd fallen into a thoughtful silence.

Suddenly he turned to Brenda. "How state-of-the-art is your computer?" he demanded abruptly.

"Web. Internet. You name it."

"Can I use it?"

"Sure."

The others began drifting to the pub, but Sarah followed Brenda and Justin to Colly's house. There Justin got to work, and soon located D and S on the web.

"I recognize some of those names," he said when he got a list of directors. "They're tough dealers."

"It *is* a powerful company," Brenda said. She could follow what Justin was doing. To Sarah it meant little except as something that was calling him back to his old world. Her heart was heavy.

There was no consolation as they made their way home. He was sunk in thought and answered her abstractedly. Sarah was dazed by what was happening. To see Haven threatened and to suspect that Justin's business instincts had been ignited by what, to her, was a disaster were too much to take in.

"Did you find anything out about this company?" Nick asked Justin. He'd gone back to the Haystack with the others.

"Only confirmation of what I already suspected. It's a juggernaut, a money-making machine."

He wouldn't say more, but retired to his own room. A few minutes later Sarah heard him on his mobile phone. She tried not to listen, but some words refused to be shut out.

"We have to move quickly... I've only just found out... I know this place well, and I've heard of several things that we can use... No, that's not good enough... Just do it. I want things to start happening tomorrow. And keep my name out of it... I have my reasons."

"What's he saying?" Nick demanded, appearing beside her.

"Hush, Uncle." She drew him into the kitchen.

"Who's he talking to? And why?"

"I don't know."

"He's trying to get in on it, isn't he?" Nick demanded, outraged. "A money-making machine, he said. And he's in the business of making money. We took him in, made a friend of him, and he's going to stab us in the back."

"No," Sarah said frantically. "I don't believe it— not now—he's different—"

"The leopard doesn't change his spots, darling."

"He couldn't do that to us, Uncle Nick. He knows what it would mean to us. There must be some other answer."

"Then why is he acting in secret? Why not tell us about it?"

"I don't know, but I won't believe the worst of him until I have to."

Yet despite the brave words she was afraid. Nick saw it in her face, and didn't press any further. Sarah stayed up late, waiting for Justin to come out and say good-night. Then he would say something that would make everything all right. But he didn't emerge from his room.

Next morning Justin had been scheduled to collect some goods from the wholesalers, but he excused himself, saying he had things to do but not what they were. Sarah refused to question him. She'd spent a wretched night, terrified of discovering she'd been living in a fool's paradise. Once she heard his phone ring, and he'd answered it immediately, as though waiting for the call. She couldn't hear the words, but she recognized the tone. It was urgent, driving, like a man making plans and intent on carrying them out. She remembered it from two years ago when his phone had often interrupted them. She thought perhaps she'd heard him say, "I'll see you tomorrow," but she couldn't be sure because she'd buried her head under the covers.

He ate his breakfast in a state of abstraction while he studied the local map. He drove off without saying where he was going, but Sarah had seen over his shoulder that he'd drawn a ring around the town of Datchworth. It was ten miles away, and the nearest rail link. Sarah made the trip to the wholesalers herself, heavyhearted. Justin had said nothing about leaving, but now it looked as if he was returning to his old haunts to look up contacts. Perhaps he would never return.

She was away two hours. When she returned she saw him at once, but her joy lasted only an instant. He was sitting on the bench by the duck pond, in earnest conversation with a man who, by his suit, had come from town. Justin didn't see Sarah, so absorbed was he in explaining something to his companion. As she watched he flung an arm out in an expansive gesture that took in the green and the whole of the vista beyond. Sarah hurried into the store and began unpacking the goods she'd collected. She was sick at heart.

"Will you believe me now?" Nick muttered.

"No," she answered fiercely. "There could be all sorts of reasons—"

"Darling, use your eyes. He's buying in. He's a businessman. You heard him—a money-making machine. Wait until the others hear about this."

"No!" Sarah seized his arm. "Please, Uncle Nick, wait until we know more. I know Justin—as he is now. He couldn't do this to us."

Nick looked at her sadly. "Do you really believe that?" he asked.

She turned away from his eyes that saw too much, including the doubt in her heart. "Promise me you won't say anything yet," she repeated huskily.

"All right, I'll stay quiet for a while. But if he hurts you again I'll break every bone in his body."

Sarah managed a wonky smile at the old man's fierceness. "He'll tell us all about it tonight," she insisted. "You'll see."

But Justin wasn't in for supper that night. He came home late, having spent the evening with Colly and Brenda.

A motorbike drew up outside the store, and the rider came in, pulling off his helmet. "Mr. Justin Hallwood," he said, glancing at the envelope in his hand. "Special delivery."

As Sarah signed for the letter he asked, "Can you tell me where to find Hanmere Lane? Bloke by the name of Norton. And Mrs. Drew, Haven Manor, and these others."

He showed Sarah a list. It contained five names, all

of them members of the parish council. She clutched the counter, feeling suddenly ill.

She forced herself to speak calmly and give the messenger directions. When he'd gone she stood staring at the envelope, trying to face the fact that the worst had happened. Here in her hand were the results of Justin's machinations, and there could be little doubt what they were. Hallwood Construction and Engineering had put in its own bid, rushing it to the councillors before the D and S deal could be complete. Yesterday's visitor must have been the representative of a bank, wanting to see the site before agreeing to the funding.

Suddenly she was swept by a wave of anger. How could she have let herself fall in love again with a man she knew to be hard, blinkered and indifferent to people? She'd believed he'd grown in understanding because her heart had longed to believe it, but the truth was he'd become worse.

Nick came in from the store at the rear. "We seem to be running out of— Sarah, what's the matter?"

"He's done it," she said in a shaking voice. "How could he? I've got to find him."

"He's out there on the green," Nick said, pointing.

Sarah dashed out, racing across the green to where Justin was standing, looking out over the fields. He was so preoccupied he didn't hear her approach.

"Are you pleased with yourself now?" Sarah asked bitterly.

"It's a bit too soon to be—" Justin checked himself and turned to stare at her. "Hey, how did you know what I was thinking?"

"Because there had to be a reason for all those secret phone calls. I didn't want to believe it. I thought you were better than that. But the leopard doesn't change his spots, does he?"

"Excuse me?" Justin looked blank.

"This came for you." She thrust the letter at him. "And the messenger had other letters for the councillors. So you can be glad things are working out as you planned."

He was hardly listening. He tore open the envelope with feverish fingers, read the contents and yelled, "Yes!" to the sky.

"I hope it's what you want," she said in a shaking voice.

"It's just what I want. This is wonderful! Sarah—" He reached out, but she backed away.

"Don't touch me."

"But, darling—"

"And don't call me darling, not after what you've done."

"You don't know what I've done."

"I know, and soon everyone else will know. And I tell you, you'd better get out of Haven while you're still in one piece. Go back to London. Pull your strings from there, and don't waste any time worrying about the people you betrayed. We've served our purpose. We put you on the road to a nice fat profit, didn't we? And after all, that's what really counts."

Justin was very pale. "Exactly what do you think I've done, Sarah?"

"Oh, please, at least admit it. You've put in your own bid for this site."

"What?" Justin stared at her, but before he could say more his attention was taken by an agitated figure running toward him across the green, waving a piece of paper and calling out in a strangled voice.

"Young man! Young man!"

Sarah turned and saw Councillor Norton, his face puce with fury. He was closely followed by a crowd of interested spectators, attracted by the excitement.

"What does this mean?" he demanded, waving the paper in Justin's face. "What does this mean?"

"I should have thought it was clear enough," Justin said, glancing at Norton's letter.

Everard Norton turned to Sarah, almost gibbering. "Do you know what he's done?"

"Yes," she said tiredly, "but don't get upset, Mr. Norton. Why should it make any difference to you which one of the—"

"Not make a difference? It ruins everything." He turned to appeal to the crowd, which was growing fast. Around the green, doors were opening and people streaming out. "He's destroyed the future of Haven. That's what he's done. Traitor! Traitor! The great vision that was to put us on the map—all gone because of some sentimental twaddle about gargoyles."

"Gargoyles?" Sarah exclaimed. "What—"

"Gargoyles," Norton shouted. He began to read from the letter, stabbing with his finger. "Building of outstanding historical interest—essential conservation—he's had the hall designated as a grade-one listed building. Do you know what that means? It can't be knocked down. There can't be a development." His voice rose to a shriek. "The whole scheme is ruined."

There was a split second of total, dumbfounded silence. Then a deafening roar went up from the crowd, and the next moment some of them had converged on Justin, slapping him on the back, shouting congratulations. Others stood still as though the news was too much to take in, but gradually realization dawned, and their stunned looks gave way to smiles of delight.

Justin reeled under the impact of boisterous approval. He seemed to be shaking hands with everyone at once, but although he grinned and thanked them he was looking at Sarah. Her hands had flown to her face as the truth had become clear. She wanted to laugh and cry for joy. Of course he hadn't betrayed them. How could she have thought that?

If only she could get him away, have him to herself for just a moment. But that was impossible. The crowd swelled as the news raced around the village. Everard Norton tried to voice his fury above the hubbub, but in vain. He was soon joined by Imelda Drew, "spitting feathers" as Colly later put it.

"So you did this?" Imelda snapped at Justin. "You've done nothing but make trouble since you arrived."

"You ought to be grateful to me," he observed. "I've saved you from having an ugly great development right opposite your front door."

She reddened and fell silent, but nothing could silence Everard. "You haven't heard the last of this," he said, seething. "We'll see what D and S has to say about your interference—"

A man in the crowd said something extremely coarse about D and S, and Everard turned on him, dancing with rage. But nobody was listening. They were all delirious with relief.

"Justin, why didn't you tell me?" Sarah was half laughing, half crying.

"I wanted it to be a surprise," he said. "I never thought you'd really believe—why should you think the worst of me? What have I done to deserve that?"

"Nothing," she said hastily. "But I know Hallwood's is big business—"

"I didn't know you knew anything about Hallwood's."

"Everyone's heard of Hallwood's," she said quickly. "And you were so secretive—"

"You should have known me better," he said seriously. "I love this place. I wouldn't do anything to hurt it."

"Not even for money?" she asked breathlessly.

"Not for anything."

Ted had appeared, bearing huge tankards of beer, one of which he shoved into Justin's hand. He demanded three cheers, and everyone roared while Justin looked both pleased and self-conscious.

After that things got out of hand. The crowd drifted over to the Haystack, some in and some outside. Uncle Nick appeared with Nicky in his arms. Parents went home for children, then settled on the wooden benches outside the pub. It was as though everyone recognized tonight as a landmark in the village's history, and wanted their children to be able to say, in later years, that they'd been there.

Everyone wanted to buy Justin a drink. He normally drank very little, but this was his night, and it was sweet to him in a way that no other achievement had been. He took only a mouthful from every glass offered him, but after a while they mounted up, and he began to look a little disheveled.

Sarah watched contentedly, Nicky sleeping in her arms, her chin resting on his head. She knew Justin's avoidance of alcohol had always been part of his ambition. He preferred to keep his wits clear with people he didn't trust, and he trusted nobody. Now the sight of him letting his hair down with his friends filled her with delight. Her moment would come later. She could wait, hugging her secret joy to herself.

At the height of the evening the vicar arrived home and found the village apparently deserted. Well-founded instinct directed him to the Haystack, where he was seized on, because everyone wanted the pleasure of telling the story again. George regarded Justin with awe.

"To think you thought of that and I didn't!" he exclaimed. "How did you effect it so quickly?"

Justin considered for a moment. He'd reached the stage where speech required careful negotiation. "Got someone down here yesterday," he said at last. "Most interested in the gargoyles—'specially that legend."

"What legend is that?" George asked, frowning.

"The one about the biggest gargoyle—how the stonemason based it on the mayor, because the mayor was dallying with the stonemason's wife."

"Dear me! I don't think I've ever heard that one before. Have any of you?"

Nobody had heard it before.

"It's funny how these old legends start," Justin declared. Solemnly he winked at George. Solemnly George winked back.

Sergeant Reg Mayhew dropped in, but observed that he couldn't drink on duty. This problem was resolved by the removal of his police jacket. Closing time came and went, and at last Reg said unsteadily, "Got to be careful, Ted. Be closing time soon. Got to obey the law."

"It's a great thing, the law," Justin observed to nobody in particular.

Everyone agreed with this profound statement, and on that happy note the celebrations began to break up. Justin managed to walk carefully home, but once there he sat down very suddenly on the sofa. He stayed there while Sarah put Nicky to bed.

"Sarah, I have a confession to make," he said when she returned.

"Yes, darling?"

"I'm intox—int—you know what I mean."

"Legless," she said tenderly.

"Absolu—yes."

"Then it's lucky I'm here to take you to bed."

They made their way along the corridor together, his arm about her shoulder. In his room she pulled the clothes off him and rolled him into bed. Since he didn't seem to want to release her, she climbed in with him.

"Oh, darling," she said, laughing, "you really did let yourself go tonight, didn't you?"

"Drunk as a skunk," he said happily, and passed out in her arms.

Chapter Eight

Justin awoke with a skull made of paper in which conflicting armies raged. Somehow he managed to get himself to breakfast, only to find Nicky smashing an iron hammer onto a steel anvil.

"Please," he begged, removing the weapon from the infant's hand. It turned out to be a plastic spoon, which Nicky was using to crack a boiled egg.

"Are you feeling rotten?" Sarah asked gently.

"Terrible."

"You should drink more often," Uncle Nick said heartily. "Then you'd be in shape for celebrations." He went down to open up the shop.

Sarah produced black coffee, dry toast and aspirin, laid them down gently before him and crept away. The perfect woman, he thought, one who knew how to care for a suffering man. Nicky retrieved the spoon and bashed the anvil again. Justin winced.

"I don't know why your mom had such a poor opinion of me," he mused, spooning egg into Nicky's mouth. "Do you know what she said to me?"

Nicky's grunt had a negative inflection.

"She said, 'The leopard doesn't change his spots, does he?' What do you think she meant by that? I mean, okay, she thought I'd put in my own bid for that site, but why had she assumed my spots were bad?" He spooned in some more egg. "You'll find out about women," he pronounced gloomily. "They always think the worst of a man. Remember, you heard it here first. How could she think I'd ever hurt this place?"

Sarah ought to have known without being told that the threat to Haven had made him as angry as anyone else in the village. That had been followed by a feeling uncannily like the one he'd had for Nicky that day in the shop. It was half tender protectiveness and half a determination to wage war against the enemy. And anyone who threatened Haven was an enemy.

By the time she returned he was beginning to feel normal again. "Sorry I passed out on you last night," he said. "I actually had other plans."

She laughed. "The state you were in!"

"Hell, don't remind me. It was a good night, wasn't it?"

"The best. They're all your friends now."

"But there was so much I wanted to say to you. You really had a rock-bottom opinion of me. Buy in.

Stab you all in the back. What have I ever done to make you think that?''

"Justin, don't hold it against me—"

"I'm not. Anyway, it was worth it to see your face when you realized the truth. I just want to know why you condemned me without a hearing."

"You're a tycoon, and you don't get to be one without knowing how to spot a chance."

"But I never told you I was a tycoon," he pointed out.

Luckily for Sarah she'd had all night to work on an escape from this trap. "I saw your picture in the newspaper at the time of your accident," she said, with perfect truth. "I've always known you were the boss of Hallwood Construction and Engineering. But I haven't told anyone else. You obviously just wanted to be one of us, so I didn't spoil it for you."

"Thanks, I'd like to keep it quiet a while longer, although that won't be for long if we're fighting D and S."

"But surely you've already beaten them?"

"Sarah, I didn't want to spoil things last night, but the battle's far from won."

"But you heard Councillor Norton. If they can't demolish the hall the scheme is ruined."

He shook his head. "D and S aren't going to give up so easily. They'll try to have that order overturned, and if they fail they'll think of something else. If I could have gotten it before the sale went through they might have decided it wasn't worth proceeding, but they own the hall now, and the land about it. There'll be another building scheme."

She stared in dismay. "We haven't really won at all, have we?"

"Not yet. We've blocked them, but there's still a war to fight."

"And you're the only one who can fight it. Justin, what are we going to do?"

"I've got a few ideas. If you'll get me an aspirin and another cup of coffee I'll be ready for the fray."

"Perhaps there won't be a fray," she said, trying to comfort herself. "Perhaps they'll just give up."

But any such hope was dashed the instant they set foot outside. D and S had already sent in its agent to rope off the green. Large signs proclaimed, Private Property. Keep Off.

"We can't even reach our own hall," Sarah said, aghast.

"Not your hall anymore, lady," observed a workman. "It all belongs to D and S. We'll soon start digging the foundations for the development."

"But you can't!" Sarah cried. "There's a preservation order on the hall."

"Oh, that! That'll be lifted in a day or two."

"Over my dead body!" Justin muttered.

The village didn't have long to wait for the next shot in the war. Leaflets were sent to every house, inviting the residents to a meeting in the hall to discuss "the present unsatisfactory state of affairs." The meeting was set for a week ahead, and during that time D and S made a show of power. Diggers, dredgers, cement mixers, all the paraphernalia of foundation digging were moved on site in readiness. They said, more clearly than words, that the company intended to go ahead one way or another.

Justin spent most of that week using Brenda's computer or the telephone. Everyone in Haven was watching, and the village seemed to be holding its collective breath, hoping their champion could slay Goliath for them.

Apart from Justin, the only other resident who felt capable of decided action was Crosspatch, who curled up each morning in a cement mixer and declined to move until nightfall. Miss Timmins, while terrified for her hero's safety, refused to shut him indoors.

"Did the Duke of Wellington hide indoors before the battle of Waterloo?" she demanded. "Did Winston Churchill hide indoors? There are times to forget one's personal safety. Crosspatch is making a stand. And so will we, when the time is ripe." Her eyes on Justin left no doubt of her meaning, and there was a ripple of agreement from everyone.

"It scares me, how much they're expecting of me," he confided to Sarah.

"But you can do something for Haven, can't you?" she asked.

"I'm going to try. Sarah, you won't hate me if I fail, will you?" Never before in his life had he admitted the possibility of failure, but nothing had ever mattered as much as this.

"You won't fail," she said firmly.

On the night, the hall was packed. It had been set up in such a way as to show who held the power. The councillors sat on the platform with three representatives from D and S. When everyone was seated a large, middle-aged man stood up. He had an oily manner and a smile like a knife. He introduced himself as Dane Hendle, the managing director of D and S, and apologized for the "misunderstanding."

"I take full responsibility for the lack of communication that led to you not being properly informed of the benefits this development will bring Haven. You put us in our place with that preservation order, and we bear no ill will. I'm sure when this evening is over you'll wish to unite with us in putting the matter straight."

He was armed with slides, charts and statistics, with which he put on a skilled performance. With most of his audience it fell on stony ground. But one voice was raised in praise.

"I'm sure we all feel the value of having such a busy man take time to explain what some of us might find difficult to understand."

Heads turned. It was Cyril Coverdale. Dane Hendle answered him in the same vein. Everard Norton chimed in, followed by Imelda Drew. The other three councillors looked uncomfortable.

"I'm sure you all feel, as I do, that the sooner this regrettable situation is resolved the better," Dane Hendle declaimed. "This hall really is not a building of intrinsic merit, and it will be comparatively easy for us to have the preservation order overturned. But I should like to feel that you're with us in this. Your signatures on a petition requesting that the development go ahead will be the greatest help—"

People were looking at Justin expectantly, wondering when he was going to do something. But he sat still, never taking his eyes from the platform. Sharp-suited young men with vacant faces were handing out papers to be signed. The glances cast at Justin became angry. Had he raised their hopes only to dash them? Some people were reaching for their pens, as though they might as well give up if their leader had deserted them.

"Er, excuse me, Mr. Chairman." Justin's voice sounded unusually diffident, but it was enough to rivet the attention of all the villagers. Dane Hendle turned a benign look on him.

"How can I help you, sir?"

"I'd like to know who, actually, is the owner?"

"The owner—as I thought I'd explained—is D and S. Yes, sir, D and S owns all this land and—"

"That's not what I meant. I'm asking who owns D and S."

There was a brief silence. Hendle's smile wavered by only a fraction. "Well, that seems hardly relevant. Now if there's no other—"

"I think it's very relevant," Justin interrupted him. "Since you're buying up these people's lives they're surely entitled to know these little details."

"As you say—little details. Trivial details—"

"Then you won't have any trouble telling me who owns D and S, will you?"

Hendle's temper frayed slightly. "That's a confidential matter—"

"But you're a public company. It can't be confidential."

The apparent diffidence had fallen away from Justin's voice. Everyone heard it, and the entire audience was silent, riveted.

"It's true, isn't it," Justin continued, "that more than half of D and S stock is owned by Breconfield Constructions?"

Hendle's mouth tightened. "Since you know that, there seems little point in—"

"And Breconfield is owned by Welby Properties. It is, in fact, the shareholders of Welby who stand to benefit from the destruction of Haven. I think the meeting might be interested in the names of some of the Welby shareholders."

Cyril Coverdale jumped to his feet. "This is irrelevant," he bawled. "I demand that this meeting be allowed to continue—"

But he was shouted down by the villagers. Someone grabbed him and forced him to sit. It was never clear exactly who'd done this, as there were so many who wanted the credit. Justin got up and faced the meeting. He was dressed in his usual jeans and sweater, but there was something different about him, an air of natural authority that made everyone listen.

"It won't come as a surprise to anyone to know that Cyril is a prominent shareholder of Welby," he said. "All this time he's posed as a friend of Haven and a good citizen, chauffeuring Councillor Norton to and from meetings out of the kindness of his heart. But you voted the way he wanted you to, didn't you, Everard?"

"That's slander," Councillor Norton spluttered. "Mr. Coverdale is a public-spirited man—"

"He's a very rich one, rich enough to sell you some Welby shares at a knockdown price."

Pandemonium. The audience was on its feet. Norton shouted "Slander, slander!" Hendle tried to regain command of the meeting, but in vain. Only when Justin held up his hand did the noise abate.

"We shouldn't blame Everard," he said. "He accepted those shares in innocence, not knowing that they made him a beneficiary of the sale he was promoting. Mrs. Drew, on the other hand, knew exactly what she was doing. Her shares were purchased three days before the council meeting at which the sale was approved."

There was another uproar. Imelda screamed something. Everard was on his feet, shouting and waving. Nobody heard them through the hubbub from the floor. At last Imelda gathered her things and prepared to go. Hendle took her arm and seemed to be trying to persuade her to stay, but she threw him off and shouted something that sounded like, "You promised me nobody could—" The rest was lost. At last Imelda snatched her arm away and flounced off the platform.

Hendle raised his hands for calm. "Can we stick to the point?" he called, through a frayed smile. "This is not the time for such matters. Young man," he said, addressing Justin, "I daresay you think you're being very clever, interfering in matters that are far outside your understanding—"

"I understand that a lot of questions are going to be asked about how your firm conducted this matter, because I'm going to make it my business to ensure that they *are* asked."

"Look, I don't know who you think you are—"

"My name's Justin Hallwood, and don't tell me you've never heard that name before. My firm wiped the floor with yours three years ago. You used very similar methods then, I recall, and they didn't do you any good that time, either."

Hendle stared. He might be forgiven for not recognizing Justin at first, but now he looked more closely, he knew his adversary, and he paled. "We own that land!" he snapped.

"But you can't do anything with it, and I'm going to make sure it stays that way. You won't get permission to demolish the hall. You borrowed money for this project, and every day you can't start work you're paying a fortune in interest. I'll fight you all the way, and I'll delay you until your interest charges go through the roof. Be wise, Hendle. Sell while the going's good."

Caught off guard, Hendle blurted the truth. "Who's going to want to buy land that can't be built on?"

"You never know, some white knight may come galloping to the rescue. Of course you'll have to sell at a loss, but that might save you from charges of fraud and corruption."

The villagers cheered him. Hendle pointed a finger at Justin and mouthed, "You haven't heard the last of this." Then he and his sharp-suited young men gathered their things and fled.

Justin stayed where he was. He was exhilarated by the approval of his new friends, but his eyes were fixed on the front row, where Sarah sat, leading the cheers. And on her lap Nicky clapped his hands and crowed.

As the roars washed over him, he knew a moment of complete happiness. This was his world, where he belonged. He felt he'd come home.

Inevitably the meeting adjourned to the Haystack. Justin stayed a while, knowing it would give offense if he wasn't there to hear the plaudits and let them relive his victory. But as soon as he could he slipped away.

Sarah had gone on ahead, and he arrived just as she finished putting Nicky to bed. They were in each other's arms the next instant. Sarah kissed him eagerly, trying to let him know not only of her love but also her admiration and thankfulness that he'd made himself a part of Haven. And in his returning kiss she could feel his need for reassurance.

"My hero," she said, laughing through her kisses.

"That's all I want to be. Love me, Sarah."

He lifted her and carried her to his room. He didn't put on the light but laid her on the bed, raining kisses on her while he undressed her and she did the same for him.

"Hey, what are you doing?" he asked, for she'd gone beyond undressing him and was letting her fingers drift along his spine in a way she knew he found exciting. She'd never dared to try his favorite caresses before, lest she betray too much knowledge, but tonight she was exhilarated to the point of recklessness.

"What does it feel like I'm doing?" she teased.

"Driving me crazy. Hey, you never did that before!"

"If you don't like it, I'll stop."

"Don't you dare. Just keep right on." The last word

was lost in a gasp of satisfaction as she found the exact place on his spine where he was most vulnerable.

"Witch!" he growled. "Where did you learn all this?"

"I can read your mind," she said, laughing.

"My mind has nothing to do with what's happening now. Come here. Damned if you're going to have all the fun!"

His hands were roving intimately over her body, exploring curves and valleys in a way that quickly drove her excitement to fever pitch. She came back at him, kissing him in ways she knew he loved. She'd meant to say so much tonight, how proud she was of him, how much she loved everything that he was. But there was nothing words could say that couldn't be explained better like this. There was no doubt her endeavors were a triumphant success. His urgency was plain, and he wasted no time rolling her onto her back and entering her while her hands continued to work their magic on him.

He was like a man inspired, and Sarah responded with a frenzy of desire. It was lust for its own sake, for they were that sure of each other now, and could enjoy the gaiety of the bed as well as its tenderness. He drove into her powerfully, and at once her legs curled about his hips, telling him that she wanted more and yet more. He obliged, using the steely strength of his hips and thighs, taking pleasure in her moans of mindless pleasure and the grip of her fingers on his shoulders that revealed her extremity. They came together, battle honors even, and lay drained and gasping in each other's arms.

"You sure know how to get the best out of a man," he said, sitting up at last.

Sarah watched him, half hoping, half fearing that the old familiar caresses would have awakened a memory, if not in his mind, then in his body. But his eyes held nothing but admiration.

"What a woman!" he said, grinning.

But as he looked at her, lying there in her glorious nakedness, his smile faded, and he lay down beside her again.

"You know it was all for you, don't you?" he said.

"And for them."

"Yes, for them," he conceded. "For George, and Colly, and Nick, and Miss Timmins, and even for Crosspatch. But mostly for you. And for Nicky. I want him to have all this so he can grow up knowing the things I didn't. And I wanted you to be proud of me."

This time his kiss was tender, and the arms that drew her close were gentler than they'd ever been.

"My Sarah," he whispered against her mouth. "Don't ever leave me, Sarah. You mustn't ever go away." He drew back, frowning. "Why did I say that? Why did I suddenly think about you leaving?"

"You're more likely to leave than I am."

"Only for a short while. I have to go to London to sort some things out with D and S, but I'll be back in a few days. You'll be here when I get back, won't you?"

"Of course I will."

"You're sure about that?"

"Quite sure," she said, and waited breathlessly for what might be coming next. A little corner of the curtain hiding Justin's lost years seemed to have lifted. He was so close....

"I don't know what got into me," he said, shaking his head. "I guess I've gone a little crazy tonight." He settled into her arms. "Could you bear to make love with a crazy man?"

"Any time, anywhere," she said fervently.

This time it was different. The laughter had faded, leaving only love behind. The merry battle was over for this night. Now there was only the sweetness of the peace, and the total joy of belonging to the man she loved. And for the first time Sarah dared to hope that joy might last forever.

Chapter Nine

After love came rest. Sarah lay wrapped in Justin's
arms, her head against his chest, listening to the slow
beat of his heart. She was totally and utterly happy.
In that other life she'd lain against him, trying to believe he shared her feelings but secretly knowing his
mind was elsewhere.

Now a dozen little signs told her that his spirit was
still with hers—the firm clasp of his arms about her
body, the soft caress of his fingers on her hair, the
touch of his lips on her forehead. She looked up and
found him watching her.

"You seemed so far away," he whispered. "I was
afraid you'd forgotten me."

Where had it come from, this sensitivity to her
slightest moods from a man who'd once noticed nothing?

"I'll never forget you, my love," she said softly. "Never, as long as I live."

He yawned. "I can't believe it's dawn already."

"It isn't," she said, snuggling against him. "Not for hours yet."

"Then what's that light in the sky?"

"Mmm?" She opened her eyes and looked where he was pointing. A light could clearly be seen through the gap in the curtains.

"It's only two in the morning," Justin said, consulting his watch. "Hell! What *is* that?"

"It's coming from across the green," Sarah said as she pulled back the curtains. "Justin, it's the hall. It's on fire!"

With an oath he leaped out of bed and pulled on his jeans. Sarah dashed for the phone to call the fire brigade. Justin reached the bottom of the stairs just as she set down the receiver. "All the local fire engines are out on calls," she said desperately. "They're going to send one from the next station, but it'll take a while to get here."

Justin swore. "Yes, of course. They've thought of everything."

"What's up?" Uncle Nick appeared on the landing.

"Someone's fired the hall and taken great care to keep the fire services occupied," Justin said.

Sarah looked aghast. "You don't mean—"

"I'll wager anything you like that those calls turn out to be hoaxes," Justin said bitterly. "It's been fixed so the fire services can't get here in time."

"It's not just the hall," Nick said. "This heat wave

has made it like a tinderbox out there. One spark will send the whole village up.''

"Surely they'll see it," Sarah cried frantically, looking out the window. "We did."

"We're closest," Nick pointed out. "And the other near houses have bedroom windows that face the other way."

"Then we'll have to do something ourselves," Justin said. "Sarah, how many buckets have you got in the shop?''

"We've just had a new delivery. Why?"

"Nick, get them out to the duck pond."

"You want me to start calling people?" Sarah asked.

"No time, I've got a quicker way." Justin raced out of the door and across the green. Smoke was billowing from the hall, and it hit him like a blanket. He covered his mouth and nose and made it to the door of the bell tower. There was no time to call on the vicar for the key. Justin went back a few steps and hurled himself at the door. It shuddered under the impact but held. Again. This time there was the sound of rotten wood splintering off rusty hinges. One more time, and the door gave way. He was in the bell tower, fighting not to breathe in smoke, groping his way to the rope. He found it, unwound it from the hook and pulled hard.

From above his head came a deep, melancholy boom. Justin tugged harder, and the boom became a clang. That should get them out of their beds! Again and again he yanked, praying that the frail timbers would hold and not send Great Gavin crashing down on him.

At last something was happening. All over the village lights came on, front doors opened and people poured out, summoned by the din. Justin's back and arms ached, his lungs were burning, his eyes were closed against the smoke. In a desperate trance he pulled and pulled while overhead Gavin bawled and bellowed exultantly, crying that his time had come again.

At last Justin heard the shouts on the green. He released the rope and staggered against the wall. He was choking, and he knew he must get out soon, but he'd lost all sense of direction. He began to feel his way along the wall, but he seemed to be going around and around, getting nowhere. He was seized with a terrible fear of dying now that he'd discovered a purpose to life.

The next moment he felt hands take hold of him.

"Come on." That was a man's voice in his ear. "Push him my way, Ted."

Two men guided him out into the blessedly fresh air. They turned out to be Ted and Colly, who'd seen the situation and come in after him. Justin heard his name called as the crowd saw him.

Nick was there, handing out buckets. "We've got to use the water from the duck pond," Justin said, choking. "We can't wait for fire engines. Form a line from the pond to the hall. Those of you who live nearest, go home, fix up your garden hoses and pray they're long enough."

Nobody questioned his right to give orders. Men and women scattered. Sarah appeared, dragging one end of a hose that was spouting water. "It's running from the kitchen," she gasped.

"Sarah, what about Nicky?"

"The Graingers have him," she shouted. "They've opened up their house to everyone's babies so that the parents can come here. Justin, tell me what to do."

"Aim your hose through that window, but don't stand any closer than you have to."

At that moment there was an explosion from inside the hall. The roof, which was mostly wood, disintegrated before their eyes. Gavin was still swinging from the force Justin had applied, his melancholy tones echoing desolately over the destruction below. A cry went up from the crowd.

"Don't think of that," Justin yelled, his face livid in the glow from the fire. "We've got to stop it from spreading."

Men and women were dragging hoses onto the green. A line had formed from the pond, and buckets were being passed hand to hand. A group of children had come to enjoy the excitement.

"Get back," Justin roared at them, but they only scattered and returned.

"All right, you lot, *move.*"

Justin stared in the direction of the new voice, full of authority. It was Joker.

"Stop mucking about," Joker yelled. "Start being useful. Make a line at the top of the bucket queue. Grab the empty buckets and get back to the pond with them as fast as you can. *Get to it!*"

The youngsters ran to obey him, and in a few minutes they'd perfected the rhythm. Full buckets were passed along the line to Colly, at the head. As soon as he'd tossed the water into the flames the bucket was grabbed out of his hand by a child who raced away, leaving Colly free to snatch up the next bucket. Joker worked harder than anyone. Just once he stopped, to steal a hopeful glance at Justin, who gave him a brief nod of approval.

After a while Colly flagged, and Justin took his place at the head of the line. He didn't know how long he was there, working blindly against an enemy that seemed unbeatable, but at last they all heard the welcome sound of a bell, and the next moment a fire engine appeared and drove onto the green. The villagers scattered to make way for the figures who leaped out, running with huge hoses toward the inferno.

"Are they in time?" Uncle Nick asked.

"Not to save the hall," Colly told him. "But to save the village—thanks to Justin."

There was a rumble of agreement, but it was drowned by an earsplitting sound from above. The timbers that supported Great Gavin had finally given way. The huge bell tore itself loose from the moorings that had held for six hundred years and plunged fifty feet, to land with a crash that rocked the ground.

In the early dawn they surveyed the wreckage. Two of the walls, made of the original gray stone, were still standing. But the roof had gone, the brickwork had fared badly, and the tower had disintegrated.

When the firefighters had time to sit down with a well-deserved cup of tea, Justin talked to them and discovered it was as he'd suspected. The call that had detained them had turned out to be a hoax. "And not just us," the chief said angrily. "There were at least three others, or you'd have had someone sooner."

Miss Timmins began to cry. "They've won, then," she sobbed.

"They?" the chief asked. "You mean you know who's responsible?"

"We know," Justin said grimly. "But I doubt if you'll ever prove it."

Colly clapped Justin on the shoulder. "After all you did for us, lad," he said. "Not just tonight, but at the meeting. It's heartbreaking to have it fail."

"Oh, no!" Justin said firmly. "The things I do don't fail."

"But there's nothing else to be done," Colly protested.

"There's nothing else *you* can do," Justin declared with a touch of the old arrogance. "But I can!"

He returned home to have a shower and a quick breakfast. "Will you drive me to the railway station?" he asked Sarah. "I'm going to London for a few days. There are things to do that can't be done from here."

"White knight?" she asked.

He grinned. "I'm keeping it as a surprise. You can think the worst of me in the meantime."

"Will I ever be allowed to forget that?"

"When we're old and gray."

He didn't elaborate, and it was a silent journey, but as they waited for his train Justin suddenly said, "Sarah, will you marry me?"

"Oh, Justin!" Her face was radiant. But the eager acceptance died on her lips. She longed to marry him, but how could she say yes until there could be complete honesty between them? There were so many things he must know first.

"What is it?" he asked anxiously. "Don't you love me? Is that it?"

"I love you with all my heart," she said passionately.

"Then marry me now. I want you to be my wife, and Nicky to be my son. I couldn't love him more if he were my own. I know I'll never quite displace your first love. A corner of your heart will always belong to him, and I guess I'll just have to try to accept that. But there's a place for me, isn't there? Not just in your heart, but in your life? Hell, there's the train."

He gave her a fierce kiss, and there was no time to say more. Sarah drove thoughtfully to Haven. Despite her happiness she could feel storm clouds coming. Matters weren't as simple as Justin thought, and who could know how everything would turn out?

Uncle Nick had no doubts. "Tell him everything," he said at once. "You should have done it before this."

"I can't do that," Sarah insisted. "It's got to come from inside him. He's got to remember me because he wants to."

"And suppose he never remembers?" Uncle Nick asked gently.

She looked away. It was too terrible to contemplate.

Justin was gone a week. By the second day there was no trace of D and S. The villagers watched, pleased but puzzled, as the company's signs were dismantled, only to be replaced a few hours later by others saying Greenfield Estates. It seemed that the heart of the village had merely passed from one owner to another, but at least the name was reassuring.

More reassurance came in the form of Jack Redham, an employee of Greenfield, who was in charge of the site. He was a young man with a friendly manner, happy to pass on what little knowledge he had.

"There was a heck of a rumpus when that hall burned down," he confided. "Somebody got moving very fast and had the preservation order slapped back on, insisting that the hall be rebuilt. D and S gave in. They've got enough on their hands with the police investigation. I reckon they were glad to sell to Greenfield for the best price they could get. They made a loss, though."

"But what are you going to do with it?" Miss Timmins demanded. "Not another shopping complex?"

"Don't see how we can if we're rebuilding the hall," Jack pointed out. "No, it's going to stay as it is, for the use of the village. But it's not going to be *given* to the village. The boss vetoed that idea. He said there'd be nothing to stop the council trying to sell it again."

There was a rumble of agreement, and several glances were cast at Everard, who pretended not to see them.

"Greenfield will be the owner," Jack continued, "but it's setting up a committee, with several villagers sitting on it, to help make the decisions."

"Very proper," Councillor Norton declared. "I

shall be happy to offer my services. You'll be needing a man of my experience.''

Jack asked his name politely, but when he heard it he shook his head. "Sorry, sir, you're not on my list.''

"List?" Norton echoed in outrage. "What list?''

"I've been given a list of people I'm to approach.'' He consulted a paper. "Miss Timmins, Mr. Nick Mottson, the vicar—''

There were delighted smiles, except from Norton, who sniffed and declared, "I daresay you'll ask that upstart Hallwood. He's a newcomer here, but he seems to think he can butt into everything.''

"Oh, no, sir,'' Jack said at once. "Mr. Hallwood said his name mustn't be mentioned—'' He stopped and clapped a hand over his mouth.

"Does Mr. Hallwood, by any chance, have anything to do with Greenfield Estates?" Miss Timmins asked.

"I wouldn't know, madam, I'm sure,'' Jack said, wooden-faced.

Nick hurried to Sarah with the news. "It's Justin, isn't it?" he said. "It has to be.''

She nodded. "I used to hate his other life,'' she said thoughtfully. "London, big business, big money, crowds and hurry. But I have to admit it's made this possible. If Justin didn't have all that behind him, he couldn't have saved us. If only—'' She broke off because it was hard to put her thoughts into words. Justin had told her little more than the others, and she was puzzled at his secrecy.

She looked in on Nicky, who was fast asleep, clutching Ger. Justin's gift was his favorite toy and wasn't allowed to leave him, night or day. Her own little bear sat by her bed, reminding her of the giver. She rubbed her cheek against it, missing Justin desperately.

He walked in one morning while she was stacking boxes. Nicky saw him first and shouted a greeting. The next moment Justin scooped the child up with one arm and embraced Sarah with the other.

In a few minutes customers began to crowd the little shop. The news had gotten around, and everyone wanted to see him with their own eyes and reassure themselves that he was really back. A series of pointed and none too subtle questions established that he was here to stay, and after that the mood became festive.

Not everyone regarded Justin with approval. To Everard Norton he was the man who'd destroyed a grand vision and given him a very awkward meeting with the Fraud Squad. To Imelda Drew he was the man who'd driven her darling son away. He was also an upstart, the owner of new, and therefore vulgar, money, who'd interfered in her schemes. And Justin soon discovered another unexpected grudge.

He and Sarah rode often these days. Their favorite ride lay across the right-of-way that ran through Merton Farm and out into the countryside beyond. But one morning they found the path barred to them. Will Merton regarded their exasperation with sour pleasure.

"If you want to go through, you gotta pay," he snapped.

"Why should we?" Sarah demanded. "It's a right-of-way."

"Gotta protect my crops."

"We've never damaged your crops, and you know it," Justin said. "What's this really about?"

"I've got a right to make a living. Can't get cash one way, gotta make it another. They was gonna pay me good money, till you come along."

Light dawned. "You were hoping for something from D and S?" Justin asked.

"They was gonna buy the farm," Will snapped. "Place is no good to me. Who wants it now? If you want to go through, pay up."

Justin handed over some cash and rode on thoughtfully.

"Of course they'd have needed this place, too," he mused. "I wonder why they didn't buy it to start with."

Up ahead they could see Merton's combine harvester being made ready for the harvest in a couple of weeks. Hal was working on it, not too happily. He looked up and waved as they approached.

"Been having your ears bent by old Misery Guts?" he asked. "It's all his own fault, you know. D and S tried to buy the farm in the first place, and he held out for a better price. He reckoned they'd have to meet him in the end. Only then the sale fell through, and he's left wishing he'd taken the money when he could."

"So that's what it's all about," Justin said.

"Yes. Like I told you before, he's a stingy old so-and-so. Won't take proper care of his machinery. This thing's on its last legs, but he tells me to get it going. I'm cheaper than a proper mechanic, aren't I? Okay, stand clear, and let's see how I'm doing."

They backed off while he got into the cabin and started the machine. It came to noisy life but didn't move. After peering out of the cabin, trying to see the problem, Hal jumped down and went to have a closer look.

At that moment the machine made an explosive sound and lurched forward. Sarah screamed a warning as one of the blades swung toward Hal. He just managed to jump aside and avoid being killed, but the wicked-looking blade slashed at his arm, and suddenly there was blood everywhere.

"Call an ambulance," Justin yelled at Sarah, leaping from his horse. He knelt beside the groaning man while Sarah spurred her horse to the house.

Will Merton's reaction to his employee's accident was all that might have been expected of him. "Clumsy idiot!" he raged. "That's an expensive piece of machinery."

"If we don't get an ambulance here soon Hal may lose his arm," Sarah cried angrily. "Where's the telephone?"

Grumbling, he showed her, then hurried to the field to find out if his harvester was damaged. Sarah stayed where she was to guide the ambulance, which mercifully arrived quickly. She led the way to the scene of the accident. Justin had ripped off Hal's damaged sleeve and used it to make a rough tourniquet. He handed over to the medics with relief.

"What about me, eh?" Will raged. "Who's going to pay for my machine?"

Hal groaned. "I'm sorry, Mr. Merton—"

"Sorry's no good to me!"

"It's a damned sight more than you're entitled to,"
Justin told him furiously. "You had no right to make
him mend that machine. If Hal's got any sense he'll
sue you."

"Me?" Will gibbered. *"Me?"* But he fell silent
under the contempt in Justin's face.

"I've got to tell Hal's wife," Sarah said as the ambulance drove off. "Poor woman, how's she going to
get to the hospital? They haven't got a car."

"Mr. Merton will be delighted to drive her," Justin
said, with a look at the man that dared him to argue.
Merton said nothing, cowed by the force of Justin's
personality.

In the end it was Sarah who drove Mrs. Jones to
the hospital, while Justin returned the horses to the
riding school. She'd expected him to join them as soon
as possible, but there was no sign of him. She com-
forted Hal's wife as best she could, but there was no
denying that the situation looked black.

"What's the point of suing Merton?" Mrs. Jones
asked bitterly. "He's such an old miser, you can bet
he hasn't kept up the payments on his insurance."

Sarah was silent. Even if Hal didn't lose his arm, it
was unlikely to regain its full strength.

At last the doctor came to tell them that the news
was good so far. Hal's arm was saved. "But it'll be a
good while before he can use it properly."

He didn't say, "If he ever can," but the words hung
in the air.

Sarah drove Mrs. Jones home, then returned the car.
She found Justin sitting in the kitchen of Will's lovely
old farmhouse, talking to him calmly. Remembering

his contempt for the man, Sarah was surprised. He rose as soon as he saw her.

"Come in," Will said, sounding almost affable. "I've got some sherry somewhere. We'll have a celebration."

"Thank you, but we must be going," Justin said, slipping his arm around Sarah and drawing her to the door.

"What's he celebrating?" she asked.

"He's just sold the farm, and he's a happy man."

"Sold the farm? Who to?"

"Me."

"But what are you going to do with a farm?"

"It won't be a farm when I've finished with it. Don't look like that. I'm not going to turn it into a shopping complex. But I've got plans. And they'll include a job for Hal, and full pay until he's strong enough to work."

"That's wonderful!" She threw her arms about his neck. "Do tell me, what are you going to do?"

"Not yet. Trust me, Sarah."

He was thoughtful on the way home. "What's the matter?" Sarah asked.

"I don't know—at least, I do, but I can't put it into words. None of this has worked out as I'd hoped."

"But you've won. You saved Haven."

"But not in the way I wanted to. I did it with money and power, and that's not— I don't know."

"Money and power are important," she said, echoing the old Justin.

"Yes, they are. But I wanted people here to accept me as a friend, not just as a rich man who happened along." He gave an awkward laugh. "I suppose I mean that I want them to like me."

"You say that as if you were embarrassed to admit it."

"Well, I may not know what I was like this last two years, but I remember myself before. Being liked didn't come high on my list of priorities. But now— these are good people, nice people. I want them to feel the same about me."

"But they liked you before this happened. It was going into that bell tower that really made you one of us."

He sighed. "I'm asking for the moon, aren't I?"

"Why not? Sometimes you get given the moon."

"I won the moon on the day you said you loved me," he said, touching her face. "Why should I want anything else? It's just that I can't separate you from this place."

She rubbed her cheek against his shoulder. "Be patient. Your chance will come."

Chapter Ten

Hal Jones was popular, and at first everyone was concerned for him. But when they were sure his wound would heal, consternation settled over the village. As usual, the mood found expression in the Haystack.

"We're sunk," Colly declared dramatically.

"Finished," the vicar agreed sadly into his sherry.

"Haven's last chance gone," Uncle Nick sighed. "Fill it up, Ted. I feel the need of strength tonight."

"Hey, what is this?" Justin demanded, while Ted filled Nick's glass. "Since when did Haven's future ride on Hal's back?"

"Not his back, his limbs," Colly explained. "Best pair of legs in the county. Thighs all muscles. Arms like tree trunks. We'd have won this year."

"Won what?" Justin demanded.

"The tug-of-war," Ted explained. "We have one every year with Eltonbridge."

Eltonbridge was a village about ten miles down the road, of roughly the same size and population as Haven. Centuries ago they'd been sworn enemies, raiding each other's crops and carrying off each other's women. All that was left now was the tug-of-war at the annual Haven harvest fete. Eltonbridge had won for the last five years, but then Hal had moved into the area. This year Haven had felt its chance had come, until Hal's accident.

"Maybe someone else will turn up just as good," Justin observed.

"We've got two weeks," Ted observed. He looked at the vicar. "A miracle would be handy."

"I'll get to work on it," George promised. "Although Haven's been blessed with so many miracles recently that I hardly like to ask for another." He nodded in Justin's direction, and the others grunted agreement.

Justin became aware that a silence had fallen. Colly, Ted and the others were looking at him appraisingly.

Miss Timmins, who was sipping a port and lemon with Crosspatch on her lap, suddenly observed, "Sarah's an excellent cook. I've often said so."

"She's terrific," Justin agreed cautiously.

"I remember you when you first came here. Skin and bone. And look at you now."

They all did so. Justin's shoulders had broadened, and hours in the saddle had thickened his thigh muscles. Feeling self-conscious under this scrutiny, he looked at himself, and realized that none of his sharp city suits would fit him now. But then, he'd grown out of that life long ago.

"Of course, it's a lot to ask of you," George said thoughtfully.

"It is. I've never been in a tug-of-war before," Justin said quickly.

George sighed. "It's been a dream of mine to coach the winning team and watch them go up for the presentation of the victory medals. They're lovely medals, you know. Ted, show him."

Ted turned to the display behind the bar where a row of metal disks confirmed that Haven hadn't always been on the losing side. "The players all get a medal each," he said. "But the team medal is hung here, so that the world may wonder and admire."

"I'm getting old," George said regretfully. "I don't suppose I'll see another victory in my lifetime."

"Cut it out, George," Justin ordered, grinning. He looked around the expectant faces. "All right, of course I'll do it."

There was a cheer from everyone in the pub. All other conversations had died as the important negotiations at the bar had become clear. Ted produced a foaming tankard. "On the house!" he roared.

Somehow the news got around Haven in a few minutes, and the other team members started to arrive. They looked Justin up and down critically, pronounced him passable and demanded an immediate trial of strength. George fetched the rope from the vicarage where he stored it with his vestments, and they lined up, three on each end.

Like many men who'd never tried it, Justin had

vaguely imagined that a tug-of-war was easy if you were strong enough. He was soon put right. The haul used muscles he'd never known he had. In a short time he was aching all over, perspiration was dripping into his eyes, and his arms felt as if they were being pulled from their sockets. But he hung on, knowing he was at a turning point in his relations with Haven.

He ended the evening on the ground, covered in dust, while George lectured him on how to dig his heels in. The rest of the team hauled him to his feet, slapped him on the back and pronounced that he'd do. Sarah later told him that this was high praise, but he'd already worked it out for himself.

That evening was the first of many. Justin found that his vision had narrowed from the wide world to a tin medal. He'd won medals before, international awards for business achievement. None of them had mattered like this one. When he'd earned it, and proved himself, he would be in a better position to demand a final answer from Sarah.

Gradually the fete became the focus for all the things that were changing in the village. Greenfield Estates had held its first meeting with the Haven committee, as it was now officially known. Miss Timmins had reported that all was well. Jack Redham, representing Greenfield, had taken detailed notes of the villagers' opinions. There was also generous remuneration for the committee members, which was particularly welcome as the price of cat food had gone up. Best of all, she was happy to report, Jack seemed to have a sense of the fitness of things. Knowing Miss Timmins's high standards, everyone relaxed after that.

In only one way had the meeting proved a disappointment. No arguments or blandishments had induced Jack to admit that Justin had anything to do with Greenfield. The farthest he would go was a nervous, "It would be more than my job's worth to tell you that, ma'am." This seemed to everyone a kind of confirmation, especially in view of the personal interest Justin was taking in the rebuilding of the hall.

Greenfield had booked a stall to display a model of the new hall. It was to be a larger building then the old, giving the Haven Players scope for their ambitions. The architect had incorporated what was left of the bell tower, and the outside was to be made of local stone, to blend into the village. Justin had personally picked his way through the burned ruins, salvaging gargoyles that would find a home on the new walls.

He'd also rescued Great Gavin. After its final triumphant effort the bell had been left misshapen by its fall. Justin had it restored, polished and hung on display at ground level. There was a plaque giving its history, including that final night when it had saved Haven.

The heat wave continued until three days before the fete, when the weather took an abrupt turn for the worse. The temperature fell overnight, and Haven awoke to pouring rain. It pelted down all day and all the following night. Next morning the sun was out again, but there was still a nip in the air.

Greg Hallwood, driving toward Haven, was dismayed to find himself going along narrow country tracks. He reflected that if he'd known Justin had buried himself in the back of beyond he wouldn't have brought his brand-new car.

It was the love of his life, one of the first of this year's registration. Justin had taught him the value of being seen in an up-to-date vehicle, and he'd rather hoped to impress his brother. Now, bouncing in and out of holes that threatened his suspension and hearing the ominous rasp of twigs on his paintwork, he regretted the decision.

It was evening as he neared Haven, and the rain was starting again. In the distance he could see lights and hear noisy laughter. As he grew closer he made out a patch of grass lit by the glow from a nearby pub. Men were on each end of a rope, straining against each other and constantly slipping on the wet ground. Around them stood a crowd, drinking beer and cheering them on.

Greg's first thought was that he'd come to the wrong place. He began to walk across the grass in search of someone to ask, wondering if he'd be able to make himself heard above the riotous jollity. At that moment the two teams collapsed as their feet slid from under them. There was more laughter and cheering. Someone yelled, "Okay, that's it for tonight!" and the men picked themselves up to head for the pub.

"Excuse me!" Greg hailed one of the muddied oafs. The man turned, grinning, and with a shock Greg recognized him.

"Justin?"

"Greg? What the devil are you doing here?"

Justin looked dismayed, as well he might, Greg thought, being caught in such an undignified situation.

It was scarcely possible. "It *is* you—isn't it?" he asked in a dazed voice.

"I'm honestly not sure," Justin said. "*You* may not think it's me." He looked around and saw they were attracting attention. "Look, come over here." He took Greg's expensively clad arm and felt his brother flinch. "Sorry," he said, making vain efforts to wipe out the muddy fingerprints.

"You're making it worse," Greg complained, tight-lipped.

"Sorry," Justin said again.

"Leave it!" Greg snapped.

"Hi, Justin!" someone called. "Coming for a drink?"

"Not tonight," Justin called back. To Greg's relief his brother made no introductions, but steered him away. "We can't talk here. Have you got somewhere to stay?"

"No. Where are *you* staying?"

"Er—there's no room for you there. Better try Market Dorsey, down the road. They've got a good hotel. I'll get cleaned up and join you in the Haystack."

He appeared half an hour later, without the mud, wearing jeans and a tweed jacket, looking more informal than Greg had ever seen him. "Shall we make tracks?" he asked without sitting down.

"Don't you want a drink first?"

"Er—no, it's getting late. I've called the hotel to book you in, but if we don't get there soon you won't be able to get a meal. I'll wait outside while you finish." He vanished.

Greg followed him immediately. As they drove he

grumbled, "Anyone would think you didn't want to be seen with me." He hadn't meant it seriously, for such an idea was preposterous, but to his astonishment Justin reddened awkwardly. "You have to be kidding," Greg said in outrage.

"Don't make a big deal of it," Justin said with a reluctant grin. "I just can't afford to be seen talking to someone in a car like this."

"But don't they know who you are, what you've done for them?"

"They know I'm connected with the land purchase, but not how closely connected. I'm trying to play that side of things down. Being seen with you could ruin my image."

"Which appears to be that of a yokel," Greg said stiffly.

"Well—let's just say that if you got a pair of jeans and drove an old banger it would be easier for me to admit you're my brother."

"I think you've gone totally off your head," Greg snapped, then added quickly, "I'm sorry. I didn't mean that."

"No problem. Take the next right turn and we're there."

They reached the Grange Hotel just in time for a meal. Greg checked his room out, changed his paw-marked suit and joined Justin in the restaurant with a heavy heart. "You're different," were his first words.

"So are you. What happened to the little brother I was always telling off for not taking things seriously?"

"You left him in charge of the firm, and it's been

a good education. I could fool around when I was your assistant, but my fooling days are over. At last I've understood the point of a lot of the things you taught me.''

''Oh, Lord!'' Justin exclaimed in dismay.

''What's that supposed to mean?'' Greg stopped as the waiter appeared with their meals. ''I didn't order.''

''I ordered for you. They want to close soon.''

''Steak and kidney pie?''

''It's the best steak and kidney for miles.'' Justin addressed the waiter. ''Tell the cook Sarah's expecting some fresh asparagus tomorrow.'' The waiter nodded and disappeared.

''What have I wandered into?'' Greg demanded faintly.

''That's the way things are done around here.''

''What about the telephone? Or hasn't it reached this place?''

''Sure. And there's a young woman in Haven with a computer that's more state-of-the-art than anything we've got. But talking to people is nicer.''

''And who's Sarah?''

''She and her uncle keep the shop where I'm lodging. I help out when I can.''

''You help out in a shop?''

''It's the least I can do after all she's done for me. I was a shadow when I walked into this place, and she got me fit again.'' Justin looked up as he saw the waiter trying to catch his attention. Under Greg's fascinated gaze, the man held up both hands with the fingers splayed. Justin returned a thumbs-up sign.

"The cook wants ten bundles of asparagus," he explained.

"Justin, what the hell were you doing back there?"

Before he could reply, Justin began coughing. He controlled it and said cheerfully, "Practising for the tug-of-war. It's the big day tomorrow. We have high hopes of beating Eltonbridge, but it's going to be a fight."

"We? You mean you and the rest of the yokels? You talk as if you were one of them."

"They're not yokels," Justin said seriously. "They're intelligent, sensitive human beings, and if I thought they saw me as one of them I'd feel honored. But I've got a way to go yet. Perhaps if I help them win I'll cross the last hurdle."

"Why don't you just tell them you bought the land?" Greg demanded. He was growing more unsettled by the moment. "Surely they'd be grateful for that?"

"I don't want it getting about," Justin said quickly. "I think they suspect, but they can't be sure. I want them to accept *me*, not my money."

"Show people a fat wallet, and they'll accept you fast enough," Greg said. "Your own words."

Justin stared at him, appalled. "You've changed more than I thought," he said. "At one time you'd never have said a thing like that."

"Does that mean your memory's come back?" Greg asked quickly.

"No, nothing's come back. But I can remember before that. You were always on at me to let people off the hook, and I used to pull you out of nightclubs because you had to be at work early."

"Much time I've had for nightclubs since you went away!"

"Did I load too much on you?"

"No, I'm fine. I enjoy it. Like I said, it's taught me how right you were about everything. I thought you'd be pleased that I've seen the light at last, and I find you sliding about in the mud like some hayseed, talking about not wanting to be seen with me."

"I was having a good time."

"And catching your death of cold."

"Quit sounding like Mom," Justin complained with a grin.

"You were always the first one to catch cold. Once, you even managed to get bronchitis in a heat wave." Greg regarded his brother with concern. "You're sickening for something now, aren't you?"

"Nonsense, I'm fit as a fiddle."

"Then why do you keep coughing?"

"Okay, okay, I caught a little cold. I'll dose myself with hot milk and aspirin and be fine tomorrow. What brings you down here unexpectedly, Greg?"

"Several things, chief of which is concern for you. This latest mad idea—Merton's Farm."

"Has that gone through all right?"

"Oh, we've bought it. At least, our subsidiary, Greenfield Estates, has bought it. I won't even try to tell you what old Benton said when he heard you wanted to rename Kwikbuild Inc. Greenfield Estates."

"I was afraid a name like Kwikbuild would cause alarm around here," Justin said, grinning.

Greg sighed. "I also understood you wanted Kwik-build sold off because it wasn't achieving its performance targets. I'd started looking for buyers, but then you change your mind—"

"Then I'm sorry if I confused you. I want Green-field for myself, my own personal baby. I'm going to take complete charge of everything."

"You're going to be a *farmer*? Then let me tell you that you haven't got the aptitude. I've had Merton's looked over. It's a mess. The place is going to rack and ruin." He stopped as a waiter approached them and began to clear away the plates. To his surprise he found he'd eaten the whole of the steak and kidney pie. It had been excellent.

Justin ordered apple pie and ice cream for them both. "But it must be Denton's ice cream," he warned. "You'll like it," he told his brother, who merely stared at him, beyond speech.

Rather to his own dismay, Greg did enjoy the ice cream, but his alarm that Justin's mind was wandering only deepened.

As if by telepathy Justin said, "There's method in my madness. I wanted you to taste that stuff so you'll understand what I'm planning."

"You're going to make ice cream?" Greg asked weakly.

"No, just to help Denton go on making it. I'm not planning to farm that place. I'm going to build small commercial units that will facilitate the making of ice cream, traditional furniture and so on. I might even take over one of the units myself—" he held up his hands "—and put *these* to some use. I'd almost forgotten that I was an engineer. Perhaps it's time to remember. There'll be a place for Joker, too, so that all that misused intelligence finds a proper outlet, and—''

Greg groaned. ''I don't know who Joker is, and I'm not going to ask, for fear of having my ear bent with any more pearls of backwoods wisdom. I'll just remind you that units that size aren't economic. You've said so yourself.''

''Not if they're on their own, but they can work as part of a greater whole. I'll *make* them economic. It can be done, with proper investment and imaginative planning. I'm going to put Hallwood's resources behind these people, get them export contracts. One unit will be a technology shop where they can hire time on state-of-the-art facilities. There'll be all the latest software. The whole countryside can use the facilities, but my people will have a generous discount.''

Something in the way Justin said *my people* made Greg stare at him, but he said nothing. He concentrated on his apple pie and ice cream to give himself time to think.

''What about planning permission?'' he asked at last. ''This is agricultural land.''

''That'll take some negotiation,'' Justin agreed, ''but I'll get the permissions I need because it'll benefit the area. There'll be jobs for young people, so they won't have to leave the village. And when your surveyor went over the farm, did he notice that beautiful house?''

''Yes, he thought it might be worth something if it was put in proper repair. You could sell that for a tidy sum—''

"I'm not going to sell it, I'm going to live in it."

"You're really stuck into this toy-town arrangement, aren't you? What about your work at head office?"

"I'll stay in overall control, but I can put the day-to-day running in the hands of a deputy."

"Me?" Greg said at once, eagerly.

"I'm not sure. I'm not happy with what you're becoming."

"I'm becoming like you."

"That's what I mean. I don't want you making my mistakes."

"Justin, you can't give this to anyone but me. I've done a good job while you've been away. Just look at the figures—"

"I'll think about it. But if I do give you the reins you'll have to put up with me looking in regularly to make sure you're not throwing any widows and orphans onto the streets." He saw his brother's face and added gently, "That was a joke, Greg."

"Joke?" Greg sounded as though his ears had deceived him. "You made a joke?"

"Why not? Other people make jokes."

"Yes, other people. Not you."

"Well, it takes practise, but I'm getting the hang of it," Justin said, a tad defensively.

"Have you told anyone down here about this scheme—raised their hopes?"

"No," Justin said thoughtfully. "I'm saving it for the right moment." He saw Greg's expression and said, "Forget it. I'm not going to change my mind. Greg, try to understand, I *want* to do this. It's a challenge. I enjoy making money, and I'm going to make it with this place. The old firm is no challenge anymore."

"Now there you're wrong," Greg declared, glad to be on firm ground again. "There's another reason I came here. I wanted to talk to you about the Hampson contract. We wanted it badly, but lost out to Sedgewick's. But Sedgewick only beat us by slashing their prices too much, and the word on the grapevine is that they can't cope. If we move fast we can still get in there, squeeze them out and take them over on our own terms."

"Then we'd be the ones who couldn't cope," Justin observed.

"Not if we slash their work force by half. With our capacity we can manage the contract on the other half."

"What about the people who'll lose their jobs?"

"Industry is rationalizing and downsizing all the time. People expect it these days."

"But how will they manage?" Justin persisted.

"It's not our problem. You can fulfill your dream of making Hallwood's the biggest firm of its kind in the country, and then the world."

"Is that my dream?"

"Don't tell me you've forgotten that, too. I've heard you talking about it for the last ten years. You used to say that only the grand vision mattered, not the details."

"But you're talking about throwing people out of work," Justin said. "Are people just details? How many small people will we have to crush to achieve this dream?''

As he said the words he had an eerie sensation, like being haunted by a snatch of a tune, heard once, long ago, an echo from another world. He rubbed his eyes.

"What is it?" Greg demanded, alarmed.

"Nothing. It's just that— Greg, did you and I ever have this conversation before?"

"I've never heard you talk like this before in your life."

"Strange. I just felt I was covering old ground. I guess I imagined it." He passed a hand over his eyes.

"You're not well," Greg insisted. "You ought to pull out of that tug-of-war."

"Are you kidding? I'm the anchor man. They need me."

"Don't you think this game has gone far enough?"

"That's all you think it is? Just a game?"

"All right, a vacation. You've enjoyed yourself among the little people, because they're a pleasant change, but now it's time to come back to the real world."

"Greg, do you think the lives these people live are any less real than yours? That they matter less because they have time for each other?"

He saw his brother regarding him helplessly, and realized that Greg didn't even understand the question, never mind have an answer.

They talked little for the rest of the meal. Each was uneasy with the change in the other. Justin longed to get home to Haven. His head ached, and he felt more feverish than he was going to let his brother suspect.

Greg drove him back and dropped him off outside the store. Justin didn't invite him in. He wasn't ready to bring his two worlds together. But as Greg was turning the car he saw the door open and a young woman appear in the light. She embraced Justin, laying her cheek fondly against his. They went into the house arm in arm. Greg was thoughtful as he drove to his hotel, and once upstairs he immediately got on the phone.

"Marguerite? Thank goodness I found you in. It's worse than we feared."

He was having the old dream again. There was the brick wall, and the mist was dragging at his feet as he felt his way along. There was the corner, with its hint that here at last he might find the answer, but, as always, the man appeared, blocking his way. But this time it was different. Instead of himself, it was Greg who stood before him. Justin awoke with a shudder.

"What is it, darling?" Sarah hurried in, closing the door behind her. "You were shouting in your sleep. Is it the dream again?"

"It's changed. The man in my way is my brother. I've turned into him—no, he's turned into me. That's what's happening to him." He pulled himself up in bed and ran a hand through his hair. "Talking to him tonight was eerie—like talking to my own ghost. He wasn't always like that. It's the firm—it's so big it does something to you, makes you forget people."

"But you can discover them again," she reminded him.

"Yes." Justin gave a brief laugh. "Poor Greg. He

thought I'd gone mad. I must make him understand, too. Luckily he's younger. He's got time to see the light. In fact—''

He stopped. He'd been on the verge of telling her about his plans for Merton Farm. It would be nice to see the pleasure in her face. But he'd resolved to wait.

''In fact what?'' she asked.

''I'll tell you tomorrow.''

''No, tell me now,'' she protested, laughing.

''It's a surprise.'' He took her hands. ''We have to talk, Sarah. There are things I want to tell you, but I want to win that medal first.''

''It's only an old bit of tin,'' she told him.

''No, you know it's more to me than that. It means everything I've discovered here, and when I give it to you—well, then we'll talk. Perhaps we'll set our wedding day.'' He saw the shadow on her face. ''You do love me, don't you, Sarah?''

''You know I love you.''

''As much as you loved *him*?''

''Much more,'' she said. ''Someday I'll try to let you know how much more. You're the man I always wanted him to be. Before we can marry I have something to tell you, too. And when I've told you, you may not want to marry me.''

''Nothing could make me not want to marry you,'' he said simply. ''Nothing in the world.'' He touched her cheek. ''Good night, my darling.''

When she'd left him he fell into an uneasy doze in which he was haunted by something that had been said that night. If only he could pinpoint it... Yes! That was it!

How many small people will we have to crush?

He'd said those words, and the sudden consciousness of having heard them before had shaken him. The feeling was there again now, more strongly than ever, maddening him with its elusiveness.

The world tilted wildly. He was sitting in the dining room of the hotel arguing with Greg—he was sitting in his London apartment, arguing with Sarah—he couldn't think how she'd come to be there, but she was looking at him from disillusioned eyes and saying that people mattered. *How many small people must be crushed?* No, that was himself. He'd said that to Greg tonight. But she'd said it too, once, long ago, in another life....

He was on the brink of a momentous discovery. The inside of his head was like a child's kaleidoscope, an unformed mass of details, but when he looked at them the right way they would make a pattern. If only...

And then the world tilted back. The pattern fell into place. He sat up, staring into the darkness with shock.

He *knew*.

Chapter Eleven

At the first crack of dawn Justin let himself out the side door and wandered over onto the green. The ducks quacked sleepily and paddled to the side, expecting tidbits, but for once he had no eyes for them. He was engrossed in his inner turmoil.

The past two years had returned to him with sudden, shocking clarity. He understood everything. Sarah was his love, and Nicky was his son. There was no other man standing between himself and her. The beloved she had spoken of with such tender longing that it had roused his jealousy was himself. Despite his behavior, her love had remained golden true. And when he'd returned to her she'd opened her arms.

A whole layer of himself seemed to have gone. It was the layer of suspicion, and once it would have made him read the worst into her silence. The thought of how much she'd known and never told him would have made him feel vulnerable and angry. But he was wiser now, and he knew, without asking, why she'd kept silent. She'd known that he wasn't ready, and she'd let him reach the truth in his own time, in his own way.

And Nicky, that strong, bright little boy, a son any man would be proud of. Free of the tricks adults used to obscure the truth, he'd seen Justin with clear eyes, instinctively preferring his father to all other men. The half glad, half painful tenderness Justin had felt was the age-old, mysterious bond of the same flesh, the same blood. And this was the child he'd wanted to destroy. Now he understood the fierceness of Sarah's refusal. She had known even then what he was only now discovering.

"Sarah." He whispered her name. It had a beautiful sound. She was his true and beloved Sarah, if he'd only had eyes to see. He'd won her love, and thrown it away, oaf that he was. But by some miracle he'd been given a second chance, and this time he'd set his feet firmly on the path that led to her.

He could remember the night Sarah had told him about Haven. It was as clear now as it had been vague then. While his conscious mind had barely noticed, some deeper part had clung to the knowledge and offered it when he needed it. It hadn't been coincidence that brought him here. His heart had known where it was taking him, and why.

"You were there all the time, weren't you?" he murmured. "All through the last two years, you were there in my heart. Part of me knew you from the first moment. Not remembered, but *knew* you were the one I needed, the only one.'' He murmured her name again, and seemed to hear her answer him. The sound of her voice was beautiful, saying his name.

''Justin!''

He looked up, realizing he wasn't imagining it. She was really there, watching him with a combination of tenderness and exasperation that seemed to him, at that moment, the very essence of love. It was the look of a wife, he realized, for that was what she was, his true wife, the wife of his heart, the wife he should have married long ago, but he hadn't understood.

''How can you be so silly as to come out here in the rain without covering up properly?'' she demanded.

''It's not raining, Sarah.''

''It *is* raining.''

To his amazement, it was. He hadn't noticed it start. The air was cold, and his shirt was already wet. The church clock struck seven. He'd been sitting by the duck pond for two hours.

''Come in at once,'' Sarah insisted.

''Quit nagging,'' he said with a grin.

''If you acted sensibly in the first place I wouldn't need to nag,'' she pointed out with irrefutable logic.

''True.'' His eyes never left her adorable face. ''I love you, Sarah.''

''I love you, too. Come in out of the rain. Justin, why are you staring at me like that?''

He didn't need to ask like what? He was staring because she looked different. He could see so many other faces superimposed on the one she wore now—

the tender, glowing look she'd given him so often in the days of their first love, the gallant smile with which she'd covered heartbreak when he broke it off, the distraught expression he'd seen a few moments before she vanished. But that was gone. Now there were only love and contentment in her expression as she stood there, chivvying him, like a wife, to take care of himself.

It was on the tip of his tongue to tell her everything. But no, he thought. First he'd win the tug-of-war medal, then he'd give it to her. He'd tell her his plans for Merton Farm, how he wanted the farmhouse to be their family home. And he'd beg her to forgive him for the past. Except that he knew she already had.

He showered and did his best to hide how poorly he was feeling. A couple of aspirin helped, and his feverish flush was covered by his tan. Nothing must be allowed to spoil today.

To his dismay Sarah had cooked him an enormous breakfast, eggs, bacon, sausage, toast and marmalade. "It'll build your strength up," she said.

"I could eat a horse," he lied in his heartiest voice. In fact, even toast and black coffee would have been an effort, but he valiantly maintained his role as a man at the peak of health. "Come along, woman. Serve it up! I'm starving." He thumped his breast, gorilla style, and Nicky crowed with laughter.

He held one of Nicky's hands, wondering how he could have missed the significance of the long fingers so clearly derived from his own. The truth had been staring him in the face all the time, but until now he hadn't been ready to see it.

His heart almost failed him when she set the enormous plate before him, but luck was on his side. Sarah had to go downstairs for a moment, and her uncle hadn't yet arrived. There was only Nicky to see him seize a plastic bag from the drawer, dump most of the breakfast inside it and hide it away. "Let's keep this our secret," he told his son. The next moment the sound of Uncle Nick's step made him sit down hastily at the table.

During breakfast it stopped raining, and a weak sun appeared. People began to arrive on the green with stalls and tents. Sarah got to work on a batch of biscuits she was making for the cake stall, while Justin and Nick went over to inspect Great Gavin in his new home, where children were busy garlanding him with flowers.

Although the fete hadn't yet begun there was no lack of entertainment. For the past week there'd been a coolness between Mrs. Drew and Miss Timmins. Mrs. Drew's prize Siamese, Princess Delphine, had given birth to a litter of four, one of which was a most un-Siamese looking black. Allegations had been made in icy, dignified tones. Crosspatch had discreetly vanished, prompting Miss Timmins to frenzied accusations of abduction and assassination.

Fortunately for the peace of Haven, Crosspatch returned, having spent a happy few days on a farm, fighting every tom in sight and increasing the black kitten population. An apology was demanded and refused. Words were said. The vicar reflected sorrowfully that the fracas was unsuited to the character and dignity of both ladies, but everyone else enjoyed it enormously.

Miss Timmins took early possession of her stall and began unpacking her store of knitted garments. A bus drew up by the green and disgorged a crowd from Eltonbridge. Some were the tug-of-war team. The rest were the band, lugging tubas, French horns and drums. They began to tune up, noisily and inexpertly. More buses arrived, bringing the Eltonbridge supporters to cheer their team on.

It was still chilly, but luckily there was no more rain, and the sun became a little stronger. Visitors began to converge on the green, determined to enjoy themselves. Joker, relishing his newfound gift for organizing, arranged helpers to transport Sarah's supplies to the stall. When the things were all gone she fitted Nicky into his stroller and locked the shop. "Come along, my little man. Let's go and see Daddy cover himself with glory."

"Excuse me!"

The vision that stood there almost took Sarah's breath away. She was a tall, very blond woman, exquisitely groomed and wearing too much jewelry. It was clear that she came from a world far removed from Haven, and without knowing why Sarah felt a frisson of fear. "Can I help you?" she asked politely.

"I'm looking for Justin Hallwood. Have I come to the right place?"

"Yes, Justin's staying here."

The woman glanced at the shop and the rooms above it. "Actually here?" she asked.

"Yes, actually here."

Fast paced, Dramatic, Compelling...and most of all, Passionate!

For the residents of Grand Springs, Colorado, the storm-induced blackout was just the beginning....

36 Hours delivers: Fast-paced, emotional stories

◆

Complex, involved plotlines

◆

Top authors

◆

and, of course, Romance!

Plus! Keepsake bookmarks

WIN A COLLECTOR'S EDITION PRINT!*

*See details in book.

Available in July 1997, wherever Silhouette® books are sold.

36 HOURS

WHEN TOMORROW IS UNCERTAIN, THE ONLY SURE THING IS LOVE.

▼ Available wherever
Silhouette® books are sold.

36 HOURS

Romance as you've never seen it before!

The citizens of Grand Springs never saw those mud slides coming— or the thirty-six hour blackout that was to follow. As the little Colorado town is thrown into turmoil, its citizens must pull together to save themselves and their community. But sometimes the most life-threatening situations can inspire the most passionate of romances....

Come and experience the 36 Hours That Changed Everything!

**Attention collectors!
All Twelve 36 Hours covers
together form a single
piece of art!**

Look us up on-line at:
http://www.romance.net
Printed in Canada 2/97

"Then you must be Sarah." The words were accompanied by a smile that might have been gracious but for a chilly watchfulness that never left the woman's eyes.

"I'm Sarah Conroy."

"I've so longed to meet you. You've looked after Justin, haven't you? I hear you've done a wonderful job. You must let me thank you from the bottom of my heart."

Dislike made it hard for Sarah to speak calmly. "I don't know why you should thank me, Miss…"

"My name is Marguerite." The woman spoke as though her name should mean something.

"I'm afraid Justin's never mentioned you to me," Sarah said.

Marguerite gave a tinkling laugh. "Didn't he? That was very naughty of him. But of course, he's not quite himself since we had that terrible accident together. I've always felt so guilty about that. You see, I was driving the car. Of course, I shouldn't have done, but that's Justin for you! When he gives you a present he wants to see you enjoy it at once."

"Justin gave you the car?" Sarah asked, trying not to let her disturbance show.

"Oh, yes. It was to mark—well, let's just say it was a very special occasion. Do tell me where I can find him. I'm just longing to see his face when I surprise him."

"He's over there, on the green," Sarah said, indicating.

Marguerite immediately hurried away. Justin was talking to the vicar. He turned as Marguerite ran to-

ward him and threw her arms about his neck in an
ecstasy of greeting, kissing him again and again. Sarah
couldn't make out Justin's face, but it was clear that
he knew this woman.

She went to her stall, trying not to let herself get
upset. Justin loved her. He'd asked her to marry him,
and he wasn't the man to fool around with two
women. But while his mind had that huge gap he was
two men. This woman came from his unremembered
life, the part that happened after Sarah had fled. There
was no knowing what she meant to him, what prom-
ises he'd made.

Justin was wishing the tug-of-war would come
soon. His fever was mounting, and the world had begun to swim around him. Marguerite's arrival, followed by Greg, had the unreal quality of a dream. He
introduced them to the vicar as "my brother and Miss
Marguerite Vanner." Marguerite's smile took on a
fixed quality at his formal description, and she has-
tened to say, "I'm dear Justin's closest friend. I've
been so worried about him."

George responded politely, but not like a man overwhelmed by charm, so Marguerite changed tack, ad-
miring everything in sight, especially the church, and
making a generous gift to the restoration fund. She
then made the round of the stalls, buying knickknacks
and generally behaving like visiting royalty. Courtesy
obliged Justin to escort her.

"Darling, whatever have you gotten yourself into?"
she asked under her breath.

Justin wished she would go away. His brain was
buzzing, and he felt he needed a lot of mental energy

to cope with this designing woman. "Why did you come here?" he asked.

"Because I was worried about you, of course. You know how bad I've always felt about our accident, and when you wandered off like that, looking so ill—well, I was just devastated. We could have gone away somewhere together, and I could have looked after you."

"I've been looked after extremely well."

"By the shop assistant?" Marguerite asked with a little trill of laughter. "My darling, you really were scraping the bottom of the barrel, weren't you? 'Oh, yes, please, I'd love to buy one of those cute little— er, I'd love one.'"

"Don't speak of Sarah like that," Justin said.

"How sweet of you to be loyal to her. I won't say another word, I promise."

"Look, we've got to have a long talk. There are a lot of things we need to get straight."

"Of course, darling." She squeezed his arm. "Why don't we go somewhere now? The beer tent, perhaps? Or that ducky little place where they're selling teas and stale buns."

Her tone had a sarcastic edge that brought words of reproof to his lips, but they died unspoken. She wasn't worth the effort. After today he need never see her again. There would be only Sarah, and the plans he'd made for his new life here.

He turned, seeking the reassurance that the sight of Sarah would give him. She was only a few feet away at the cake stall, concentrating on arranging her wares. Justin went to stand in front of her. "It's going well, isn't it?" he asked, trying to sound hearty.

"I've never known it to go better," she said brightly. "Are you all ready for the fray?"

"Lead me to it."

"We're all rooting for you."

Marguerite's tinkly laughter reached them. She was throwing hoops at a stall and giggling at her mistakes. "I see she found you all right," Sarah observed.

"Have you met Marguerite?" Justin sounded displeased.

"Yes. She told me it was her fault you had an accident."

"She was driving the car."

Sarah longed to ask if the car had really been his gift, and why, but pride held her silent.

Marguerite was hopping about on one foot, having lost a dainty sandal in the wet ground. "I'd better go and see nothing happens to her," he said.

Marguerite hopped toward him and clutched his arm, full of fluttery charm. "Look what I've done now, darling," she said, and swayed, obliging him to put his arm about her. He said something Sarah couldn't hear, but she heard Marguerite's answer well enough.

"I think they're all too quaint and charming. Just like a picture postcard come to life, only not quite real, if you know what I mean. Honestly, some of them ought to be wearing peasant smocks—"

"Cut it out, Marguerite," Justin said wearily. His head was thumping, and it was an effort to speak. "These are good people, and that sort of remark only gets their backs up." Inwardly he prayed for the day to be over soon. He wasn't sure how much longer he could keep upright.

"Well, what do you care?" she snapped. "You know as well as I do that you don't really..." The rest was lost as Justin led her away.

For the first time Sarah noticed how cold the wind was. There'd been something wrong with Justin's manner. He'd reproved Marguerite for her insensitive comment, but only halfheartedly. There'd been none of the passionate affection she'd come to believe he felt for Haven. Others had noticed, too. Haven villagers were looking at each other in bewilderment.

Sarah served customers calmly for the next hour, then it was time for the tug-of-war. Justin appeared with Marguerite in tow. "Wish me luck," he said to Sarah.

"Go in and win for us all," she said.

"I'm going to win that medal. You'll see."

"Will the teams line up, please?" The words came over the loudspeaker.

"Right, this is it."

"Let us both give you a kiss for luck," Sarah said. She needed the reassurance that he would be prepared to kiss her in front of this other woman.

He was about to kiss them, but then Nicky reached toward him and something shouted a warning in Justin's head. The child, so small and precious, and himself, a mass of flu germs. It would be unpardonable to give his illness to either of the two he loved, but the baby especially. He jerked back as fast as he could.

"They're calling me," he said hurriedly, and departed, giving her hand a squeeze to let her know that no rebuff had been intended.

Sarah never felt it. She stayed rooted to the spot, trying to come to terms with the fact that Justin had snubbed her rather than let Marguerite see them kiss.

Justin took his place at the head of the team, trying to remember everything he'd learned, but things were becoming a blur. Three things stood out in his mind—Sarah, Nicky and the vital importance of the little tin medal. Marguerite blew him a kiss. He didn't even see her. But Sarah did.

"Take your places."

Haven faced Eltonbridge. Eltonbridge faced Haven. Hands on the rope. Feet in position. *Haul.*

At first Justin could hardly believe he'd done this before. It was like the first time, only worse. His body was a mass of feverish aches. Then he got a grip on himself. His legs seemed to find their strength as he dug into the earth and strained backward.

The crowd had gathered around them, cheering and shouting encouragement. Haven's cheers turned to wails of dismay as Eltonbridge managed to get back a few feet, nearly dragging Haven over the line. But at the last moment Justin dug his heels in and stopped the rout. The sudden halt jarred painfully through his body, but he managed to keep going. He was aching all over, on fire, blind, deaf, but something drove him on to the greatest effort of his life.

Bit by bit Haven drew back. Their rivals fought them for every inch, but once they'd started going forward they couldn't stop. The Eltonbridge leader's feet slipped closer to the line. His teeth were bared, his body straining, but he was struggling against a man fighting for his life, and he didn't have a chance.

Justin felt the victory creeping nearer. One more effort, just one more...

A deafening roar went up as Eltonbridge crossed the line and collapsed in a heap. Justin was drained, gasping, too weary to fully appreciate what had happened. But people were dancing about him, slapping him on the back, yelling, "We've won! We've won!" And at last he understood.

He searched frantically for Sarah in the crowd. Surely she and little Nicky had seen his moment of triumph? But the mass of faces seemed to swim before his eyes. He was wet and there was a chill wind, but his body was on fire. He tried to clear his head, wishing it didn't ache so, and looked again for Sarah.

"Justin, dear—"

There was a light hand on his arm, a beautifully modulated voice—but it wasn't *her* voice. He turned and tried to speak, but the raging fever seemed to be consuming him, and the next moment he collapsed into Marguerite's arms.

She screamed but seized him instinctively. It was the grip of a woman who'd almost let her property slip through her fingers, but wasn't going to make the same mistake twice. Greg helped her lower his brother to the ground.

"He's ill," she cried. "Get an ambulance."

Greg hastily got out his mobile phone and began to dial. People were crowding around, voicing their concern.

"We should get him inside," George said, shouldering his way forward. "Take him into the vicarage quickly."

Sarah dropped to her knees beside Justin, calling his name frantically. He half opened his eyes, and his lips shaped her name.

"We won," he murmured.

"Yes, yes, never mind that now. Darling, what's happened to you?"

"Just—a little chill—wanted to explain—"

"Explain what?"

"Everything—you were right—not to tell me—best this way." His eyes closed.

Marguerite had been favoring the vicar with her most gracious smile. She turned in time to see Sarah with Justin, looking at him with an expression that told her love as clearly as words. Marguerite saw his lips shape her name. The next moment the tug-of-war team lifted him and bore him to the vicarage. They laid him down on the huge sofa. Sarah tried to reach him, to kneel beside him and hold his hand, but she found the place already taken by Marguerite, as of right.

"The ambulance is here," Greg said, from the window.

"Thank goodness!" Marguerite cried theatrically.

George pulled open the door, and in an instant the ambulance crew were inside the vicarage. Justin was fast slipping out of consciousness. Sarah watched frantically as he was lifted onto the stretcher and carried out. She followed, but Marguerite was ahead of her, climbing into the ambulance.

"I'm coming with him," she told the crew. "He's my fiancé."

The doors slammed, hiding Justin from sight. The next moment the ambulance was moving, taking him away from Sarah, standing there, staring in stunned disbelief.

"What are you doing?" Uncle Nick demanded. "Why didn't you go with him?"

"That woman—she said he was her fiancé."

"And you believe her?"

"I don't know. Do you think he could have been lying to me all this time—treating me as a diversion?"

"Is that what you really think?" Nick demanded, more fiercely than he'd ever spoken to her before.

"No," she cried. *"No."*

"Nor do I. I was pretty much agin him when he first arrived, but I've changed my mind. I won't believe the worst of Justin until I hear it from his own lips. Come on." He started to walk purposefully.

"Where are we going?"

"We're going to follow that ambulance. They must have gone to the county hospital, so we'll catch up there."

The Graingers took charge of Nicky, and in a few minutes they were in the car and on their way to the county hospital. "Uncle Nick, what do you think is the matter with him?" Sarah asked wretchedly. "I didn't even know he was ill. How could I be so careless?"

"Don't blame yourself. He was doing his darnedest to hide it from you. He didn't eat much breakfast this morning. He threw it away when he thought neither of us was looking. That was some act he was putting on."

To her relief the county hospital was soon in sight. The minute Nick stopped the car Sarah jumped out and ran up the steps.

"Can you tell me where Mr. Hallwood is, please? It won't be there," she added quickly, as the receptionist consulted a register. "He can't have arrived more than a few minutes ago."

"Ah, yes, I know who you mean. No, he's not here."

"But he must be—I saw the ambulance take him away."

"But when he got here there was another ambulance waiting, a private one. He's been taken away to some private hospital."

"Which one? Where?" Sarah asked frantically.

"Somewhere in London, I think they said."

"London," Sarah said faintly.

"She's done it!" Nick exploded, arriving at the desk. "That woman's kidnapped him, that's what she's done."

Sarah clutched the desk as her world collapsed about her. Justin had been spirited away, and she didn't know where to start looking for him.

"And really I don't know what her parents were thinking of to send her to me." Miss Timmins sighed. "As though I'd know what to do with a surly fifteen-year-old. She doesn't want to be here. She wants to be in town with her boyfriend, though how she got a boyfriend when she never seems to wash and wears her hair in rats' tails, I don't know."

Sarah came out of her unhappy reverie. "I beg your pardon?"

"I was telling you about my great-niece, Elsie Smith, who's landed on me like a very unwelcome visitation. She's my sister's granddaughter, and the family packed her off here to get her away from a *most* undesirable young man. She's rude, sulky, never helps in the house, and the sooner she goes, the better."

Sarah forced a smile and tried to sound interested, but it was hard to keep a cheerful face when she was full of fear and misery. A week had passed since Justin had been whisked away from her, and in that time she'd had no word from him.

Nick had driven to the main library in Market Dorsey and looked up private hospitals in the London yellow pages. He'd returned armed with a long list, and they started to telephone them one by one. But some places denied that Justin was a patient, while others refused to disclose whether he was or not. He might have vanished into thin air.

She'd considered all the possible reasons for his silence, none of them comforting. If he was well enough to contact her he must have decided not to. Perhaps the return to his old world had diminished his image of Sarah, turning her into a vacation romance. Her mind bravely faced the possibility, but her heart refused to believe it. Or maybe his memory had returned, and he was angry with her for concealing the truth.

But the worst thought of all was that he was too ill to contact her, too ill even to ask someone to do it.

Somewhere the man she loved might be dying, and she couldn't find him.

When Miss Timmins had left there was only the vicar waiting to be served. "Still no news?" he asked sympathetically. Sarah shook her head.

"I'm sure you'll hear from Justin any day. And when you next see him, perhaps you'd like to give him this." The vicar held out a small metal disk. "It's his winner's medal," he explained. "Naturally the ceremony was a little muted after what happened, but the medals were distributed, and it's only right that he should have his."

When George had gone Sarah studied the cheap medal, thinking how much it had meant to Justin, what it had symbolized about his relationship with Haven. Now he'd gone, and perhaps he would never know that he'd achieved what he'd wanted so badly.

"Sarah!"

She looked up sharply as Uncle Nick came hurrying into the shop, waving a newspaper. "Read that," he said, indicating a headline. It read, Tycoon in Mercy Dash—Fiancée's Bedside Vigil.

"'Socialite Marguerite Vanner spoke tearfully of her love for tycoon Justin Hallwood, stricken with pneumonia and lying critically ill in St. Luke's Hospital, London. "He was so happy about our forthcoming wedding," she said. "And then he became ill. But hopefully he's on the road to recovery."'' Forthcoming wedding, my foot!" Nick said trenchantly. "He was no more planning to marry her than fly to the moon. You don't believe that taradiddle, do you?" he demanded of Sarah.

"No," she said slowly. "No, I don't. If it *is* true—he can look me in the eye and say it. But I don't think it's true. I think he loves me as I love him. I know where to find him now. St. Luke's Hospital."

"Are you going there?" he asked, looking at her curiously.

"Yes, I'm going." Sarah's head went up, and her eyes focused on something only she could see. "I ran away once before," she said quietly, "but I'm not going to run away this time."

Chapter Twelve

The journey to London seemed to take an age. Nick had insisted on coming, too, like a guardian angel, which had meant a last-minute flurry to find someone for the shop. Miss Timmins, who'd helped out before, agreed to take charge, but only if Elsie could be there, too.

"I daren't let her out of my sight," she confided.

Elsie had turned out to be a surly, unappealing girl, wearing clothes too short and tight for her well-rounded figure. She loathed her present banishment, and had clearly decided to be as unhelpful as possible. Nick sighed and let it go. He was far more worried about Sarah.

He drove the hundred miles to London with one stop for coffee. Sarah sat beside him, with Nicky in his car seat in the back.

Neither of them knew that section of London well—and it took three hours to find the hospital, tucked away down a side street and not looking like a hospital at all. "I've got to park the car," Uncle Nick said. "You get on in there."

Sarah took a deep breath and hurried in, holding Nicky in her arms.

The inside wasn't like her idea of a hospital, either. With its thick carpets and decorated walls, the reception area might have been the foyer of a luxurious hotel. The receptionist, a glossy young woman, looked up. "Can I help you?"

"I've come to see Mr. Hallwood."

"Your name?"

Sarah gave it, and saw the faintest trace of disturbance on the woman's face. She knew then that Marguerite had warned them of her coming.

"Will you take a seat, please, while I call someone?"

Sarah stepped back, but she stayed on her feet, and the moment the receptionist glanced away she moved quickly through the nearest door. She had no idea where it led, but instinct warned her to get as deep into the hospital as possible.

She was lost. All the elegant corridors looked like each other, with their beautiful pictures, their discreet wall lights. Then a pair of glass doors ahead of her opened, and Marguerite stood there, barring her way, her face bearing a smile of implacable graciousness.

"Miss Conroy, how lovely of you to come all this way to ask about Justin. Unnecessary, but charming."

Over Marguerite's shoulder Sarah could see two white-uniformed men, standing firm.

"I haven't come to ask about Justin, Miss Vanner," she said. "I've come to see him. I know he wants to see me."

"Oh, my dear, if only it was possible for you to see him. He's been far too ill to receive visitors. In fact he's been unconscious."

"So that's why he hasn't—"

Marguerite realized her slip and recovered quickly. "Of course, I don't mean he's been unconscious all the time, just most of it. Recently he's been awake and talking quite clearly. And he's never once mentioned you." Her eyes met Sarah's, as bland as a baby's. "I'm sure you'll understand that I have to be very protective of him, and that's why you must leave."

Sarah said nothing. She even backed a few steps as though getting ready to depart. Then, without warning, she moved to one of the chairs by the wall and sat down firmly. Her chin was set.

Marguerite came and sat beside Sarah, her face a mask of compassion. "I really think it would be better for your own sake if you went away," she said gently. "It can't do your poor baby much good to be hauled about from pillar to post." Behind her sweet smile her eyes flashed malice. "I wonder who his father could possibly be," she murmured.

Sarah met her eyes. "I think you know very well who his father is," she said. "And that's why I'm not leaving. I'm staying here until I've seen Justin."

"I'm afraid that's impossible."

"Miss Vanner, you'd better know something. Justin asked me to marry him."

Marguerite's smile became more unbearably gracious. "My dear, I'm sure he did. Justin is an impulsive man."

Once Sarah would have flinched before these tactics, but not now. In her hands she held not only her own happiness, but also that of her son and the man she loved. And for their sake she could be strong.

"I'm not going," she repeated.

"It's so sad to see you taking this attitude," Marguerite said softly. "It's not doing you any good. Justin and I have been engaged for ages."

"I'll believe that when he tells me himself."

"But you're not going to see him," Marguerite said in a voice that had a slight edge.

Sarah gave a small, mysterious smile. It was incredible, even to herself, that she could smile under these circumstances, but a sense of power was coming to her. Marguerite might seem to hold all the cards, but it was she who possessed Justin's love. And the proof of it was in her arms right now, reaching out sticky hands to Marguerite's elegantly coiffed hair.

"You must be very afraid of Justin seeing me," Sarah said. "That means you know the truth."

Marguerite's lips tightened, and she dodged to avoid Nicky's fingers. "I have nothing to be afraid of," she snapped. "Justin is engaged to me. The car in which we had the accident was his engagement gift."

Sarah looked her in the eyes. "I don't believe you."

"Are you calling me a liar?"

"Yes," Sarah said simply. "I am."

"In that case, you force me to do something I would rather have avoided."

"Do your worst. This is Justin's son, and I'm the woman he loves. And nothing you say will ever change that."

Marguerite signaled to the two men. "You're trespassing on private property," she said. "I'm giving you a last chance to leave quietly. If you don't take it, I shall have you thrown out."

"I'm staying here," Sarah said. She looked at the two men, both of whom seemed uneasy, and smiled. "I think you're both nice people," she said. "You're not going to start manhandling a woman with a baby, are you?"

"Well, if you'd just leave, miss—"

"But I'm not going to leave. And you're not going to touch me." She never raised her voice, but the resolve that radiated from her seemed to weaken their wills.

"Get her out of here," Marguerite snapped.

"That could be a problem," the older man said.

"There's no problem, just throw her out."

"But she's not causing any disturbance," the younger one objected. "Why not just let her stay?" He grinned at Nicky, who was pulling at his buttons. He had a six-month-old daughter of his own.

"I want her out," Marguerite said through gritted teeth.

At that moment a white-uniformed nurse appeared. "Miss Vanner, Mr. Hallwood is awake and is asking for you urgently."

Marguerite's face was triumphant as she rose and followed the nurse. Sarah stared after her, sick at heart.

"Wouldn't it be better if you just slipped away, miss?" the younger guard pleaded.

"Not for me, or for Justin, or for Justin's son."

"This is his son?" The young man paused delicately. "Does he, er..."

Into Sarah's mind came the memory of Justin murmuring weakly a few seconds before he passed out.

You were right not to tell me—best this way.

Did those words really mean he'd remembered everything? Was she reading too much into them?

"Yes," she said. "He knows."

Justin had regained consciousness several times, enough to recognize Greg and Marguerite hovering by his bed. But he felt too ill to do more than exchange a few words with them before drifting off again. He understood that he was in the hospital, with pneumonia, but he couldn't understand why Sarah wasn't there. She said she loved him. She'd borne him a son. Why wasn't she here?

At last he awoke with a clear head. A young nurse, tidying things near the window, looked up and smiled at him.

"How long was I out?" he asked.

"You've been delirious for several days. Don't you remember anything?"

"Only vaguely. I've lost all sense of time. What day is it? Have you got a newspaper or something?"

"Here's one your brother was reading last night." She handed it to him.

It was hard even to lift it in his weakened state, but at last he managed it, and his eyes focused on the words, Tycoon In Mercy Dash—Fiancée's Bedside Vigil. He had to read them three times before their full import reached him. Then anger gave him strength to crumple the newspaper into a ball.

"Is Miss Vanner in the hospital?" he demanded in a hard voice.

"She's been with you all the time," the nurse said sentimentally.

"Fetch her here, please, urgently."

Marguerite appeared a few moments later, smiling. But the smile faded when she saw the rage on Justin's face.

"How dare you put such a thing in the paper!" he snapped. "Did you really think you could bounce me into an engagement? You were never more mistaken."

A moment ago she'd been radiant in victory, but she faltered before his cold anger. "It—was a mistake," she said. "The reporter just assumed we were engaged, and I was too distraught to put him right."

"'He was so happy about our forthcoming wedding,'" Justin quoted ironically. "If you were saying things like that I don't wonder he 'just assumed' we were engaged."

"But, darling, what does it matter?" she asked, recovering a little. "Everyone knew we were planning to marry, even though we hadn't made an announcement. Why, we'd be husband and wife now if we hadn't had the accident—"

"If you hadn't half killed me with your stupid recklessness," he corrected grimly. "It's no use, Marguerite. I'm sorry if I led you to expect a proposal. Somehow I could never get the words out, and now I know why. I was in love with someone else all the time.''

"Well, you kept mighty quiet about that," she snapped. "All the time you were courting me—"

"I didn't deceive you on purpose. I didn't know I was in love with Sarah—I tried not to love her, but I couldn't manage it. Part of me always knew I belonged to her and that one day I'd want to reclaim what I'd thrown away—her and our child. I went to Haven because she was there, although I didn't know it at the time.''

"I think you must be wandering in your mind," Marguerite said coldly.

"No. I was once. But I'm at the end of my wandering now. I'm going to marry Sarah. I just hope she hasn't seen this announcement. What must she be thinking of me? Has she called?''

"There hasn't been a word from her," Marguerite said deliberately. "Are you sure this touching little romance isn't all in your mind, Justin?''

"She may not know where to find me. I don't suppose you told her, did you?''

"This newspaper will have told her. It's yesterday's. She's had more than twenty-four hours to make contact—but she hasn't bothered," Marguerite said, looking at him calmly.

"She may not have seen it," he said, but even as he spoke he knew he was clutching at straws. In Haven everyone knew everyone else's business. It only needed one person to see that announcement, and Sarah would know in minutes.

"Just go, please," he said quietly. "I'm sorry for our misunderstanding, but it's better if we don't see each other again."

She met his eyes and found them implacable. All her most devious weapons had proved useless. Now she could only hope that her last spiteful effort would do some real damage. Tight-lipped, she turned and left the room.

By the lift she met Greg. "I was coming to find you," she said. "That woman from Haven has turned up—Sarah Conroy or whatever she calls herself, and she's got a child she claims is Justin's. It isn't his, of course. He says he never met her until a couple of months ago, but she's been pestering him. He wants you to get rid of her."

"Right!" he said grimly, and stepped into the lift.

Marguerite waited until the lift had gone down. When she was sure there was nobody to see her ignominious defeat, she slipped quietly down the back stairs and out by a side entrance.

As soon as he was alone Justin seized the telephone and tried to recall the number of Mottson's store. But he'd never needed to call it before. He dialed an operator and a young woman asked, "Which town do you require?"

"Heaven," he said, seeing Sarah's face. Then, hearing her gasp, he laughed shakily and amended it. "Haven. Mottson's General Store."

At last he had the number and dialed it. The phone was answered by an unfamiliar voice. It was young, female and surly.

"Yeah?"

"Who's that?" he asked, startled.

"Elsie Smith," Miss Timmins's great-niece said. "Who wants to know?"

"I want to speak to Sarah Conroy."

"Ain't here."

"Mr. Mottson then."

"Ain't here."

Justin drew a breath. "Can you tell me when they'll be back?"

"I dunno. Gone, ain't they?"

"What do you mean, gone?"

"I dunno. Just gone."

"What about the baby? Did they leave him with the Graingers?"

"Dunno who the Graingers are, but they took the baby."

"But you must have some idea—"

"Look, it's no good asking me. They're all gone. That's all I know." She hung up.

A terrible fear had taken hold of Justin. It was happening a second time. Sarah had disappeared, just like before, because she thought he'd let her down. He should have told her everything he'd remembered at once. Now it might be too late. He'd been given his second chance, and he'd blown it. This time she could be lost to him for good.

"No," he said through gritted teeth. "I'm damned if I'll let it happen again."

"Miss Conroy, I'm afraid I must ask you to leave."

Sarah looked at Justin's brother but made no move.

"I'll go when Justin tells me to," she said.

"He doesn't want to see you, and he certainly isn't going to fall for any idiotic claim that this is his child. You'd never met him before he went to Haven—"

"I met him two years ago, at the Carter Vernon reception."

Her words gave Greg an uneasy jolt. He'd spent hours going over that reception, wondering why Justin's memory had shut off just a few hours before it. Suddenly he felt the ground shifting under his feet. He sat down beside Sarah and spoke in a gentler voice. "How did you come to be there?"

"My boyfriend took me. He worked for you. But he abandoned me there, and Justin took me home."

Greg remembered someone saying Justin had left with a woman. He'd thought it must be Marguerite, but Justin had said no.

"I know his memory stopped the day before," Sarah went on, "so when we met again in Haven he didn't know me. But something he said recently made me think he might have remembered."

"What did he say?"

She shook her head. "I can't tell that to anyone."

"Look, I don't want to be hard, but I've only your word that this is true. Marguerite says he told her he didn't want to see you."

"Mr. Hallwood, do you really take everything Marguerite says as gospel?"

Despite himself Greg couldn't repress a slight smile. "If you put it that way, no. But Justin's been very ill with pneumonia. He nearly died. I can't take any risks." He ran his hand through his hair. Like the security men, he was coming under the effect of Sarah's personality, with its calm force that would accept no refusal.

"Couldn't you go away and come back tomorrow?" he asked. "If you need money——"

"I'm staying here until I see him. Mr. Hallwood, you're not going to throw me out."

"Aren't I?"

"You're not even going to try."

Her assurance was disconcerting. "I see. You think you know me?"

"Only what Justin's told me about you. The night you came he was upset because you were growing too much like him, but he said there was still time for you to change back."

"Justin told you *that?*" he asked, slightly aghast. Subconsciously he was relaxing. Whatever the truth about this, Justin knew her well enough to confide in her.

He looked at the child. Nicky stared back from eyes of the deepest blue Greg had ever seen, except in one other face. Nicky waved a friendly hand, and Greg took it absently into his. Through the infant pudginess it was already clear how long the fingers were going to be—as long as Justin's one day. He made up his mind.

"Up that flight of stairs, at the end of the corridor," he said, pointing.

Sarah flashed him a smile of gratitude and ran up the stairs. At the top she found herself at the end of a long passage lined with doors, but she kept her eyes fixed on the one facing her at the very end.

And as she watched, the door opened and a man appeared, walking very slowly, as if with a huge effort.

"Justin!" she cried.

He stopped. It had taken all his strength to dress and get as far as the door, but he'd forced himself on, driven by the fear of losing her and Nicky again. Now he wondered if he was hallucinating. The woman who was calling to him down the length of the corridor had an unreal quality, like the woman who'd called him in the feverish dreams of the last few days. He waited as she grew close and her outlines became firmer. The child in her arms gave a shout of joy at the sight of him.

She stopped a few feet away, as though hardly daring to believe it was him. "You've remembered, haven't you?" she asked breathlessly.

He nodded, smiling his recognition and relief. He hadn't the strength to do more, but no words were needed. Each read the truth in the other's eyes.

Then Sarah knew what she must do. Setting Nicky gently on the floor, she took something from her bag and pressed it into his hands. It was the tug-of-war medal. "Take this," she said. "Give it to Daddy."

Justin never took his eyes from his little son as the child sturdily toddled the few steps toward him and held the medal up. The next moment Sarah ran forward, and the two of them were folded into Justin's arms, never to leave them again.

Neither of them noticed Uncle Nick appear at the

far end of the corridor. He stood watching, smiling contentedly. At long last he'd found something of true beauty, as he'd always known he would.

* * * * *

Share in the joy of yuletide romance with brand-new
stories by two of the genre's most beloved writers

DIANA PALMER

and

JOAN JOHNSTON

in

LONE STAR
CHRISTMAS

Diana Palmer and Joan Johnston share their favorite
Christmas anecdotes and personal stories in this
special hardbound edition.

Diana Palmer delivers an irresistible spin-off of her
LONG, TALL TEXANS series and Joan Johnston crafts an
unforgettable new chapter to **HAWK'S WAY** in this wonderful
keepsake edition celebrating the holiday season. So
perfect for gift giving, you'll want one for yourself...and
one to give to a special friend!

Available in November at your favorite retail outlet!

Only from

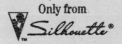

Silhouette®

Look us up on-line at: http://www.romance.net   JJDPXMAS

Take 4 bestselling love stories FREE

Plus get a FREE surprise gift!

Special Limited-time Offer

Mail to Silhouette Reader Service™

**3010 Walden Avenue
P.O. Box 1867
Buffalo, N.Y. 14240-1867**

YES! Please send me 4 free Silhouette Special Edition® novels and my free surprise gift. Then send me 6 brand-new novels every month, which I will receive months before they appear in bookstores. Bill me at the low price of $3.34 each plus 25¢ delivery and applicable sales tax, if any.* That's the complete price and a savings of over 10% off the cover prices—quite a bargain! I understand that accepting the books and gift places me under no obligation ever to buy any books. I can always return a shipment and cancel at any time. Even if I never buy another book from Silhouette, the 4 free books and the surprise gift are mine to keep forever.

235 BPA A3UV

Name	(PLEASE PRINT)	
Address	Apt. No.	
City	State	Zip

This offer is limited to one order per household and not valid to present Silhouette Special Edition® subscribers. *Terms and prices are subject to change without notice. Sales tax applicable in N.Y.

USPED-696

©1990 Harlequin Enterprises Limited

Bestselling author

JOAN JOHNSTON

continues her wildly popular miniseries with an
all-new, longer-length novel

The Virgin Groom

HAWK'S WAY

One minute, Mac Macready was a living legend in
Texas—every kid's idol, every man's envy, every
woman's fantasy. The next, his fiancée dumped him,
his career was hanging in the balance and his future
was looking mighty uncertain. Then there was the
matter of his scandalous secret, which didn't stand a
chance of staying a secret. So would he succumb to
Jewel Whitelaw's shocking proposal—or take cold
showers for the rest of the long, hot summer...?

Available August 1997
wherever Silhouette books are sold.

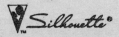

Look us up on-line at: http://www.romance.net   HAWK

From the bestselling author of
THIS MATTER OF MARRIAGE

DEBBIE MACOMBER

Their dreams were different and their life-styles clashed, but their love was anything but mismatched!

Chase Brown offered Letty Ellison love and a life with him on his ranch. She chose Hollywood instead. Now, nine years later, she's come back with her young daughter—another man's child—and as the past confronts Letty and Chase, they must learn that some things are more important than pride.

DENIM AND DIAMONDS

Available August 1997
at your favorite retail outlet.

"Debbie Macomber is the queen of laughter and love."
—Elizabeth Lowell

 MIRA The brightest star in women's fiction

Look us up on-line at: http://www.romance.net   MDM7

New York Times bestselling author

LINDA LAEL MILLER

Two separate worlds, denied by destiny.

THERE AND NOW

Elizabeth McCartney returns to her centuries-old family home
in search of refuge—never dreaming escape would lie over a
threshold. She is taken back one hundred years into the past and
into the bedroom of the very handsome Dr. Jonathan Fortner,
who demands an explanation from his T-shirt-clad "guest."

But Elizabeth has no *reasonable* explanation to offer.

Available in July 1997 at your favorite retail outlet.

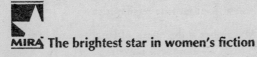

MIRA The brightest star in women's fiction

Look us up on-line at: http://www.romance.net

MLLM8